LIVVY TAKES
THE
LONG WAY

BY
ELSA KURT

LIVVY TAKES THE LONG WAY

ELSA KURT

@authorelsakurt@gmail.com

Ordering Information:
Quantity sales. Special discounts are available on quantity purchases by corporations, associations, and others. For details, contact the publisher at the address above.
Orders by U.S. trade bookstores and wholesalers. Please contact authorelsakurt@gmail.com or visit www.elsakurt.com.

Printed in the United States of America

Cover Design: Fantasia Frog Designs

LIVVY TAKES THE LONG WAY

CONTENTS

LIVVY TAKES THE LONG WAY

ACKNOWLEDGMENTS

As always, my first and greatest thanks go to my husband. Without his constant encouragement & support, writing would've remained an unrequited love. To my dear friend Jen who has had my back from day one, thank you.

This is a work of fiction. Many of the characters are composites of people I've known in my life, and some events have parallels to events in real life. Writing Livvy was a labor of love and release, and will always hold a place in my heart.

LIVVY TAKES THE LONG WAY

ELSA KURT

"Forgive me pretty baby/but I always take the long way home…"
-Tom Waits

LIVVY TAKES THE LONG WAY

PROLOGUE

Once there was a little girl who grew up like so many little girls — reading fairytales about princes, knights in shining armor, damsels in distress, and so on and on. She loved that world. She loved it so much more than her real world, the one with distant fathers and work driven mothers that she retreated to that magical place whenever possible. As she grew, she secretly continued to dream and imagine that the handsome prince would save her from her boring life, and she would live happily ever after. No one ever told this little girl that fairy tales were just that. Nothing more and so much less. No, this little girl had to learn the hard way and the long way that if she wanted to be rescued, she'd have to do it herself. And so, she did. This is that little girls grown up story...

LIVVY TAKES THE LONG WAY

ONE *WATER STAINS*

12:34 P.M.

That look. I can feel your eyes on me. Those boring brown eyes. I hate your face. I do. You keep looking at me and all I can I think is, 'I hate your fucking face.'

But I don't glance up. I don't say that. I never say the thoughts in my head.

The oscillating fan blows one strand of flyaway hair in my face and I re-tuck it for the hundredth time. I should switch seats, but it'll only provoke him more. It's hot. Shirt-sticking, sweat-beading kind of hot, the kind not usually synonymous with mid-May. I lift my eyes up in time to see a shiny bead of sweat roll down his temple.

The central air broke last August. No one will come out to fix it until mid-June because *I* forgot to call the guy back in March like *he* told me to. Thanks to this week's unexpected high temps, he hasn't let me forget that fact. Why let it go when he can come up with a thousand ways to remind me I screwed up? My husband is not the kind of man who lets *anything* go.

Kadee and I love the heat, but it makes him even more miserable than usual. I glance up — furtive, rabbit-like — from the corner of my eye. He's peeled half the label off his beer.

I hate when you do that.

Those damp little snowflakes of paper. They'll dry up, stick to his garish new cherry wood table, and I'll be the one to scrape it off later that night with a dull butter knife and cello sponge. New scratches on finished wood, and a water stain too, because I'll be too tired to get a damn paper towel and wipe it all up after. Whatever, though. I don't like the table. I would have preferred the rustic farmhouse style but Brad and his mother decided on this one. This shiny, showroom floor monstrosity with matching upholstered chairs, china cabinet and buffet.

So, here we are, sitting at the ugly table, Brad at the head, me on the side closest to the kitchen. I'll give it another minute or two. Make it seem like I'm invested in this non-conversation we're having. Then I'll come up with an excuse to go outside again. I can't breathe in here, and it's not because of the heat. It's because of *him*. Bradley sucks the air out of every room he inhabits. I'll tell him I need to run back to the garden. I don't, not really. The garden needs no more tending today, but *he* doesn't need to know that. Hell, I'll just go sit on Kadee's swing, rock back and forth and kick up a little dust until he goes upstairs for a nap. Thinking of the garden reminds me of something. There *was* something else I could do to get away from him. What was it, damn it? Remember, Livvy, remember.

As is typical, the only conversation happening between my husband and I is in my head, and it's more like a monologue. It is the one we'll never have *outside* of my head. Bradley Handler doesn't *do* conversation. In the beginning, I don't know, I guess I didn't notice. That sounds crazy, I realize. When we started out we were a couple of kids. Well, I was. Seventeen going on eighteen, to be exact. Playing grown up, like it was some kind of big fun.

But like life always does, it got real. Not so fun anymore. Those things he did? The constant joking, the one-liners, those things? Yeah, they stopped being funny. Just like my mom said they would. By now, I suppose it's obvious I want out, off this merry-go-round. Yet, I'm not leaving. Where would I go? Back to my mother's? It's about my only option, far as I can see it.

Anyhow, Kadee loves that swing out in the deep backyard about as much as I love my little patch of dirt trying to be a garden in the back corner. That's how I persuade myself to stay put, like a good girl. A swing and a garden.

Let me backtrack. For the past three days, while Kadee takes her naps, I've been digging the whole thing by hand — all ten by fifteen feet of it — using a shovel and manual tiller.

Today, as I rake it into a tidy rectangle, he comes sauntering out the screen door, and laughs that loud fake bray of his as he shakes his head, saying, "You have no idea what you're doing, do you? Why can't you just go to the grocery store like normal people?"

He's home early. Last I knew, he was supposed to be at the main office in Plantsville till two o'clock. But now he's home, disrupting my peace. An ice pick of fear shoots through my brain. Did he get fired? Please, don't let that be the reason he's home. Instead of answering, I just dig harder.

Oh, Bradley, how I want to whack you across the face with this shovel.

I keep my head down, so he can't see me smirking at the image in my head. He'd want to hear what's so damn funny, and well, I might have to tell him.

That'd be another fight. So, I keep digging and tilling and raking it all out even though it's done because if I stop while he's still standing there, we'll have to talk. Or I'll hit him with this dirt caked shovel. There's half a worm stuck to it, still writhing, and even while half my brain tries to un-see it, the other half is picturing it mashed against his cheek.

My silence pisses him off. I hear it in his tone when he tells me, "Take a break and spend time with me for once."

Tells. Not asks. My blood boils.

Not looking up, keeping my voice neutral, I say, "No time to stop, Kadee will wake up from her nap any time now."

Silence. Then, like he expected I would, I put down the shovel with a loud sigh and follow him back into the house. I glare at the wrinkled white dress shirt stretched tight across his back and sneer at his fat ass in his khaki slacks. When he turns his head back, I rearrange my face back to its glacial calm. My quiet, stupid acts of rebellion.

He shouts over his shoulder as he walks in, his voice scraping through the quiet house and out into the yard like nails on a chalkboard. *Shouting* even though the back door leads right into the kitchen, even though I'm only ten steps behind. He jerks open the refrigerator door, rattling everything inside.

"Havin' a beer. It's hot as balls in here."

Ah, always classy, Brad, always classy. One of your special skills. For your next trick, you'll suck the air out of the room.

An internal monologue, this one like a wildlife documentary, plays in my head as he lumbers down the hall to the dining room.

And here we have the gorillis humanis, note his sloping forehead and stubby hands. These particular primates are characterized by their typically demeaning, critical, and condescending grunts. They are also known to have mood swings, characterized by petulant, childish whining, and/or passive aggressive undertones. They are most adept at deliberately working every last nerve of their partner and seeking the most offensive way to do just about every single thing. Note how he engages in combative and destructive behavior to get a rise from his mate.

Anyone who knows me, I mean truly *knows* me, understands that the wrongest way to get what you want from me, is to order me to do it. At least, that's how it was with the old me.

The 'me' before you, Brad.

It's the Bradley specialty. Passive-aggressive bullying, with a hearty dash of condescending critique. Lucky me. There have been times when I wondered if he doesn't realize he's doing it. I mean, does he *really* do it on purpose? Then I remember. He does. He likes it, the reaction he gets — seeing my jaw clench and my temper simmer below the surface. Given it's the only time he ever sees any emotion from me towards him, he does it on purpose.

It's all irrelevant, I suppose, because now, instead of peacefully digging in my new garden, I'm sitting diagonally from him in his sweat-stained and button strained dress shirt and listening to his blunt fingernail scratch at that stupid label, waiting for him to say something.

I am a caged lion, pacing. Back and forth. Back and forth. I can hear the birds outside, the neighbor's chocolate lab, Cocoa. So original, I wryly think, because I think things 'wryly' all the time now. A side-effect from life with the great Brad Handler. Further off, the warbled carnival song of the neighborhood ice cream truck. That asshole comes around twice every day, the second time is always before dinnertime. Jerk.

As ever, Brad is too loud, too hyper, shattering the easy calm in the house like a thousand glasses crashing to the floor. Once again, I shush him. *The baby is sleeping*, I say. Kadee is not a baby anymore. Not really. She's three years going on four in a matter of months, all long blonde hair and three-year-old attitude and cute as hell. I hope he does wake her up. Then I'd have an excuse to avoid him.

"Relax, her door's shut. Just sit with me. Act like you want to spend time with your husband, will ya?"

Great. Fucking great. Sit with him, so we can say nothing of relevance. If I don't come up with something quick, he will suggest we go upstairs for sex. I would rather eat the dirt I was just raking before he came home and ruined my day.

So you know, I wasn't always like this, this mean-minded woman I've become. I remember the 'used-to-be' me. The 'me' I was before him. I was fun, relaxed. Laid back, even. And I still am. Just not when he's around. No, when Bradley is home, or we're out together, I'm tense. On guard. Wary and weary.

Sure, I put on a good show, or try to at least. My problems are no one else's business, thank you very much. Hell, we both put on our shows. Him, the exaggerated cartoon character buffoon, making inappropriate jokes, not-so-subtle innuendos, and playing to the crowd. Mr. Jolly, Mr. Self-Deprecating.

I play my role. The beleaguered, but ever good-natured, tolerant wife. I shrug my shoulders, *'wada am I gonna do with this guy'* expression planted firmly, and whisper a couple, *'he's teasing, don't worry'* placations to the more visibly appalled. I'm the Alice to his Ralph, the Abbott to his Costello, the straight man to his funny man. Only, it's not funny anymore. Was it ever?

Maybe it never was, and I was too naïve. No, too dumb to realize it. I can admit I grew up sheltered. I only had two boyfriends in high school. Nice enough guys, but they were vanilla, and I wanted someone more exciting, more, I don't know, Jubilee Roll. Instead, I got Rocky Road.

I remember the 'you' you were, Bradley.

That's even easier to do because he's the same as he as was then.

Points for consistency, Brad.

He never evolved. He is still a knuckle-dragging caveman. Damn it, that's mean again. I'm angry, that's all. I'm terminally angry these days.

Not that it's not true, though. Unfortunately for me, I can't say any of this because he'll act like a wounded bear, and somehow, I'll feel like shit. But if I could be mean out loud and not feel guilty?

I'd say, *Bradley, you're a God damn Neanderthal.*

In four and a half years, we haven't had one single intellectual conversation. Not one. Does he even *have* deep thoughts? I wouldn't know because he's never voiced a single one. God knows I've tried.

Once, I asked, "Bradley, do you believe in God? Like really believe?"

"I dunno, yeah I guess," said Brad.

I persisted. "Well, what do you believe, exactly?"

"Um, well… I believe you should blow me. How's that?"

He followed it up with a few more stupid, crude comments, and that was the end of that. Sometimes I wonder, if he couldn't say all the vulgar things he says, what *would* he say? Is he happy? Why does he love me? What does he even want out of life? I can't imagine him answering any of those questions. He'd be rendered mute if he couldn't respond, 'I'll be happy when you shut up and go burn some dinner.' Or, 'Who says I love you, dummy?' Or, 'What I want is the damn remote, go get it.'

Here's the thing. It's not totally his fault. He's talked like that from the day I met him. That was his sense of humor. There were no surprises here. So, what the hell attracted me to him, right? I guess I liked that he was so different from me. No one in my family talked like that. We were polite, proper. Mannered, self-contained… boring. Also, I was barely eighteen when we first dated. Small-town girl, no life experience. He was twenty-two, about to turn twenty-three and with no more life under his belt than mine. What we had in common comprised one thing. We were both townies.

Even though he'd gone to my high school and his reputation as a wild and crazy guy preceded him, I'd never met him. I didn't know his story until later. Much later.

When I looked at Bradley Handler, I said to myself, 'Well, there's that Jubilee Roll to my vanilla life.' That was all I saw in the beginning, all I noticed. Now here we are four years later. A very bumpy, volatile four years. Married with a child after six months of dating. I got my Jubilee Roll, didn't I?

When we found out I was pregnant with Kadee, we did what seemed obvious. We got married on a rainy March afternoon in a rented hall by a tired-looking Justice of the Peace. Me in a department store dress hiding a tiny little bump, him in a rental tuxedo, in front of about thirty friends and family.

My father, stiff and proper in his tailored suit, walked me down the makeshift aisle. As he nodded and smiled at the guests, he whispered, "It's not too late to change your mind," right before we reached the rented wedding arch where Bradley, his brother the best man, and my maid of honor, Sarah stood waiting.

I never told you that part, but it's true, Brad. My rigid, conventional Dad offered me an 'out' from marrying you.

It's also the most expressive Edward Perry has ever been in my lifetime. We danced, cut cake, did all those wedding things people do. We honeymooned in the Catskills, where it rained the whole time, and I slept more than anything else. I remember little from that week; it was all a blur.

In July, Kadee entered the world and gave me a new purpose. I fell head over heels in love with the tiny little human the instant I laid eyes on her. Everything about my sweet girl was perfection. I remember thinking as I gazed down at that little face that our life would be perfect. One month later, I turned nineteen.

Sometimes, I feel like I'm watching it all from above. Exactly like they say in books and in the movies. Just looking down like a ghost on this thing called my life. I had no idea whether it was a good idea or the worst, but I chose to marry Bradley Handler. I figured that with Kadee coming that had to be a sign it was right. And he and his mom, well, they kind of steamrolled the whole thing. I scarcely had to think at all. I only had to smile and look pretty and go along. So, I did.

My parents were too polite and reserved to say much of anything. They disapproved, no doubt, but also figured I would charge ahead, headstrong and determined to do what I wanted regardless. Even if they were the types to meddle, it wouldn't have mattered. I wanted this life I'd envisioned, and I would have it. But, now here we are.

I can't stand your mother, and I can't stand you, Brad.

Worst of all? I can't stand me. So, now what? Well, nothing, that's what. He hasn't a clue about what I'm thinking. He never does. No, he's sitting there with that label half torn off, along with his tie. I need to get out of this house, or I'll scream. It comes to me that niggling something at the edge of my mind. The Garden Club.

I blurt out, "Well, love to sit and chat, but I have that thing. The Garden Club? Remember?"

Instead of waiting for me to explain why I hate him and don't want to be married to him one second longer, he's waiting for me to justify why I had to join another volunteer group — this one at a church we don't even belong to, no less — when I could *'just stay home with him and Kadee instead.'*

14

"Why is this the first I'm hearing of this 'garden club'? What the hell are you doing that for?"

I lead with, "I *told* you, but you weren't listening," lie, then straight away follow it up with, "and because Mary and Jan said they need more volunteers. I'm home all day with the baby, it's not like I'm *not* available, Brad."

"What, so are there guys helping with this stupid thing? Is that why you want to do it?"

"Seriously? Don't be an ass. It's a church group. They are digging a community garden. Jesus, why do you always have to go there?"

"What. I'm just *ask*ing. It's only a *quest*ion. I don't see why you have to get mad. Don't you want to spend time with us?"

"Oh, my God. Brad, I'm home all day, all the time. I'm around. Anyhow, I already committed, so I can't back out now."

Okay, truth? Until now, I had no intention of going to the church thing. But sitting here, getting wafts of his piney cologne and sweat, and looking across the table at his fat fingers pick-pick-picking the label, I'm certain I might scream if I don't get out of here. But he doesn't know that.

Oh, if only he'd have texted on his way home, I could've had Lisa from next door watch Kadee and gotten out so much easier, but instead, I have to practically beg for permission. I hate it.

You love to surprise me like that, don't you Bradley? Keep me on my toes as you'd say. Asshole.

I hate that I have to justify something so innocent. He hates it that I have a life outside of the house, outside of him. We both wanted me to be a stay-at-home mom for Kadee, but I now realize it was for different reasons. I wanted to be 'that mom.' The one my mother was always too busy working to be, the PTA mom, the hands-on mom. *He* wanted to keep me in lockdown, away from the rest of the world. Well, I got what I wanted, and so did he. Mostly.

All our interactions now feel like games of war. We are two combatants strategizing ways to win every battle, waging our warfare with words and silence as weapons. I've used my first tactic — stubborn heel digging — he's used up two of his traditional tactics. Bullying followed by guilt. Next up, angry silence. That's actually my favorite. That one I can ignore, or at least pretend to. I guess it's funny in a warped way, our different fighting styles. I'd call him the girl and me the guy. He gets all emotional whereas I get cold and indifferent. Total role reversal. I called him that once — a girl — back in my feistier days. I mean, he *is* the stereotypical girl. Moody, sensitive, needy, clingy. All those things men like to claim women are.

To your credit, Bradley, you came back with a good one.

"You're too much of a bitch to be a guy," he's snorted.

I actually laughed out loud when he said that. He was as surprised as I was, but then he had to take it too far and say something disgusting. Something like *'now be a good bitch and do what bitches do best'* and it involved being on all fours, if I recall.

I peek up only once as he stood. He takes off his tie — the one with the grease stain I deliberately didn't point out this morning — and drops it on the table. It slides off and falls to the floor with a whisper.

I know you saw it fall, Bradley. Just like you know I'll be the one to pick it up.

I'll pick up the damn tie right along with his sweat-smelling shoes. One is by the front door, the other by the dining room doorway, his briefcase on the foyer floor, and the gum wrappers that fell from his pockets when he emptied them. Sometime tomorrow, I'll discover one or both of his black dress socks wedged between the cushions of the couch while I'm looking for Kadee's lost Barbie ballerina shoes. God damn things were a menace. What kind of asshole makes accessories that small? I guess the same asshole that makes dolls disproportionate and unrealistic, so girls can grow up thinking that's what they're supposed to look like, that's what kind of assholes. I sigh. I sigh a lot.

You're such a fucking slob, Brad.

If Jan were here — which she'd only be if *he* wasn't — she would say, "Well, why the fuck do you clean up after him?"

The answer is simple, "Because who the hell else is going to do it?"

I counter argue in Jan's voice, "Oh, now be honest Livvy. You're only talking to yourself here, aren't you?"

Another sigh. "Fine. FINE, you know why? Because I don't want to hear his fucking mouth. The snide comments, the attitude. It's not worth it, okay? Happy now?"

Happy. Layered word, that one. The thing is, yes, I am sort of happy. Happy in this house, with this great little kid, this stuff, this *life*. Except for One. Small. Detail.

Or big, technically. Five-foot-nine, two-hundred and sixty pounds worth of big. Give or take. It was hard to say, he'd put on 'baby weight' right along with me. I lost it all, he hung on to it, and we never *ever* talked about it. I can hardly remember what he looked like thin. When I look at old pictures, it's weird to see him so different. He doesn't like to see them, so I put them away in a cabinet under the end table in the living room.

Anyhow, he still has the same buzz cut dirty blond hair, same dark brown eyes. His long narrow nose sits the same way it always did over his thin lips. He's just... fleshier. I try not to care, not to let it bother me, but it does. It kind of pisses me off though. I mean, what the hell? I take care of myself, take pride in my appearance. Why can't he? Put in a little effort, get odor eaters for those shoes. *Try*, damn it. Jesus, I mean, he doesn't even *smell* good.

You know how that makes me feel, Bradley? Like you tricked me.

Five years ago when he was lean and still trying to impress me by dressing neatly and putting on cologne. That was all a ruse. Like some kind of bait and switch. The whole easy-going jokester persona? An illusion. A mask. Again, I remind myself; it was there all along,

I simply didn't see it. Underneath those jokes there lies a hostile, angry man.

But I can take blame too, I'm not above reproach. I *saw* the signs, the little hints and red flags that all was not as it seemed. The whole jealous/possessive thing that reared its ugly head from day three — day *three* — of dating? I considered it sweet, in that way young girls are stupid enough to believe. '*Aww, he must really love me,*' I actually thought that.

Let me fake vomit as I think about it now. I remember what started the jealousy thing, too. Ok, I suppose it didn't *start* it, but it sure added fuel to the fire. Dan fricking Bannett. His best friend, back in the day. He used to say things like, '*Dude, how'd an ugly fuck like you get with a hot chick like this one?*' And Bradley? He'd laugh, shrug exaggeratedly, and say, '*I dunno man, guess it's cuz I have a big dick.*' It mortified me, but I was also just a stupid kid, trying to hang with the big boys, so I pretended I found their crude humor funny.

Even more stupid? I took it as a compliment. Ate it up, even. I was a 'hot chick.'

I liked being the swan to your ugly duckling, okay, Brad? I admit it.

Besides, he didn't seem to mind. Not at first, at least. But later, well, later was a different story. Somehow, it was always my fault.

"Do you like Dan? I bet you do. Hey, I got an idea, you should date him, instead. I saw the way you two looked at each other, laughing at me…"

On and on it would go. For hours every time. Substitute the name 'Dan' with 'guy in the coffee shop,' 'guy in the mall,' or 'our neighbor Phil.' Or basically any man in the vicinity of our small universe. According to Bradley Handler, they're all looking at me, and they all want me.

So, I learned quickly how to stop those comments before they gained any traction. The method is simple. Don't make eye contact. Don't hug and avoid even a handshake if possible. In his mind, it all suggests something else. It's not worth the aggravation. And so now here we are — several years and a little girl later — in our big house and him making good money selling drugs.

I'm aware you hate when I say that to people, I can see the steam come out your ears when you clarify, 'Pharmaceutical Rep. I'm a Pharmaceutical Rep. Top sales rep in the state two years running.'

Then there's me, a stay-at-home Mom, baking cookies and volunteering. This is supposed to be great. I am supposed to be happy. Ah, there's that word again. Happy. Why the fuck am I not... that word? Why is it so damn complicated?

TWO *GRAB THE KEYS AND GO*

1:16 P.M.

Bradley has stomped up the stairs. I'm still at the table, staring at the flecks of paper, the empty beer bottle, and the water ring around it. I'm debating. Do I go upstairs, tell him I'm leaving for the church and peek in on Kadee?

Or do I tip-toe to the foyer, down the hall to the kitchen, clutching my keys and purse to my chest, and sneak out the back door? I feel torn. I want to see Kadee before I leave, but if she wakes up, it'll be hell trying to get out the door without her in tow. He'd like that. Then he wouldn't have to 'babysit' while I go out to 'play.' Bradley's words, not mine.

I can hear Jan's voice in my head again, "Tell that fucker you don't babysit your own damn kids." That makes me smirk a little. Thinking of Jan and her take-no-shit attitude, I sneak out the back door, grab my shovel, rake, and gloves and dash to the car like an escaped convict. When I get to the stop sign at the end of the street, I text a big fat lie to Bradley.

Had to go, looked like
u were sleeping. K's snack
and sippy are in fridge.
No cookies, plz.

Fine, so I'm not at Jan's take-no-shit level yet. But I'm working on it, Bradley. I'm working on it.

THREE *CHURCH LOT AND MICKEY'S*

1:30 P.M.

Fifteen minutes later, and with no text back yet, I pull into the wide church parking lot. There are a half dozen cars there already, two I don't recognize. The rest belong to Pastor Ted Stellar's wife, Barb. Jan, Karla Hansen, and Mary O'Malley, my dear friends. I feel my face relax for the first time since Bradley's car pulled into the driveway at home. This will be fun. From three car lengths away,

"It's about fucking time you got here. Oops, sorry Barb." Jan hollers.

I laugh — another first of the day — as Mary swats Jan's arm. Karla looks anxious and out of place in her designer overalls and wide-brimmed straw hat. She was at least ready to look the part. Mary, God bless her, has on white tennis sneakers and a pale peach cardigan over a white shirt, and matching peach Capri pants, no less.

These ladies are not gardeners. However, they are good sports. They are also my best friends. Despite having grown apart after high school, our same-aged daughters have reacquainted us over Thursday's Community Center playgroups, and those playgroups have evolved into almost daily get together's while the husbands work, or golf, or whatever they do when not around us.

"Hellllo, ladies. Everyone ready to get dirty?" I call out, waving my shovel for emphasis.

Ahh, I am *free*. Alive. Relaxed. None of the things I feel when Bradley's around. But I will not give another thought to him, or talk about him, while I'm here. Nope, not happening.

"So, how the hell did you get out of the house and get drizzle drawers to do some parenting?" Jan asked.

"Ja-*annnn*, don't ask that." Mary admonishes.

Karla adjusted her hat, and says, "Well, I for one, am glad we're doing this. It's nice to help the community."

We took a moment to realize that she was a beat behind in the conversation, but it was the perfect distraction, and I didn't have to answer Jan's question. Not that she would forget. We would somehow sneak in a bottle of wine over Mary's house after we finished, and then she would get the details she knew were to be had.

Barb is stuttering and waving to get our attention — she's been trying for several minutes — and introduces us to the two people I don't recognize. A bird-like woman with short gray hair, and a Ray-Ban glasses wearing,

26

handsome and fit looking older man. A vaguely familiar handsome, fit, older man.

"Livvy, dear, Mary, Karla... *Jan*, this is Laurie Scott. She and her husband bought the Bernstein house over on Bender Road. And this is Jack, he just moved from over... oh, well, never mind that. Ahh, thanks for joining us Jack, we can use some brute strength here today, right? Right. Okay, let's begin. I was thinking we..."

Barb droned on, too chipper as usual. But Jack distracted me. I *do* recognize him. He removes his sunglasses, and when I realize he is returning my stare, I do what comes naturally. I look away. Jan is staring at me with one raised eyebrow and a don't-even-think-about-it expression on her face. I squint back at her, and without a word spoken, tells me with that face, '*You know what.*'

Yes, I know what. Jan is noticing the superficial obviousness. Jack is good looking. Like *really* good looking, even from four car lengths away it's noticable.

I think all these things at once, What if Bradley drives by, worse, pulls in? I said there were no men working on the garden. Wait. No I didn't *say* that. Maybe I implied it, but I never said it. Phew, exonerated. Fuck, who am I kidding? He will have a shit fit over this.

Fucking great. I vow to stay as far away from the now very familiar Jack and head towards the designated plot with the others, putting myself on the farthest end, away from him. From beside me, I hear Jan mutter. Like she knows something. I ignore her and keep walking. I also ignore the thoughts in my head — the jumble of anxiety laced images of Bradley showing up and embarrassing me, and the urge to glance over at Jack. Mostly, I succeed. Until Jan opens her mouth.

"Who is this Jack guy? Kinda hot, right? Bitty Barb got herself all flustered back there, too. Ya notice?"

Mary nods sagely, "Oh, I know who he is. His youngest is on Holly's soccer team. He's the assistant coach. Now, I'm sure I've talked about him before, no? He's the one with the three daughters. Oh, and the two oldest both have soccer scholarships. Now, let's see, he's an architect. Or is it accountant? Whatever, it starts with an A…. and he's just finalized his second divorce, I heard through the grapevine, but I don't like to gossip. I hear he's renting a house over on Bartlett Street. Across town, off West Street, I believe. Anyhow, I suppose he — "

Jan throws her hands in the air, "Okay, okay, got it. Jesus, you're like the fricking mayor here. All I had to say was who's this hot Jack guy, and you magically spew his life story. Is there anyone you don't know?"

Their bickering sounds distant in my ears. Old memories come flooding back. After a pause, I say, "Weller. God damn. Jack fricking Weller. Do you guys remember when I worked in Kiddie Korner when we were in high school?"

Jan moans, "Oh, Christ, Livvy, how could we forget *that*? It was all you ever talked about, the kids are so cute, I love the — oh, my… GOD. Tell me that is *not* hot daycare dad Jack? It *is*. Holy fucking shit, it is, isn't it?."

It sure as shit is.

I tell Jan, Mary and sort of Karla, who's only half listening, "Yup. That's him all right." Then under my breath, "Fucking great."

28

I ignore Barb's 'language, ladies' stare, and keep hacking away at the dry dirt. Who starts a community garden with only six volunteers, anyhow? Bored pastor's wives, that who. Who joins in? Bored housewives, that's who. Or wives avoiding their husbands. I talk to Bradley in my head again.

I bet you'll find out because you will pull in this parking lot at any second.

I'm sweating, and it isn't just from the heat.

What the fuck Bradley, I'm not doing a damn thing wrong, and I feel guilty. Another thing? It's ridiculous that I talk way more to you in my mind than I ever do out loud.

That makes me chuckle, and Jan catches it. With a raised pale eyebrow creasing her beet red forehead — *Jesus Jan, you're Irish, put on sunblock* — she asks, "So, you gonna talk to hot daycare dad, or what? He's been staring at you as much as you've been avoiding looking at him."

I shrug. No. Yes. Ugh, I guess. I'm not approaching him, I tell myself that much. I'm guessing he recognizes me. Remembers me. I don't suppose I appear all that different from back when. My hair's lighter and longer — a little help, a little neglect — and I'm actually thinner than I was as a teen, even after having Kadee. Stress will do that, I guess.

From the quick glances I give, he looks mostly the same, too. Definitely grayer at the temples, but still fit. He has a groomed beard now. It hides the dimple that drove all the girls crazy back then. That's what threw me off. Still in the hot dad category though.

If my quick math and memory is right, I was seventeen when I first met Jack Weller, which was only five months before I met Bradley. His youngest, Macy, was the one I watched in the daycare center. Wow, if she's on Mary's daughter's soccer team, that makes her eleven now. Crazy.

She was a cute kid. All three girls were. The mother was type A, always micro-managing, always tense and in a rush. She drove everyone nuts, including her handsome husband. Jack was the total opposite, easygoing, down to earth, and did I mention really good looking?

Everyone, me included, wondered how the hell they stayed together. So, it was no big surprise when they showed up all serious and business-like in the middle of one day and closed the office door for a private meeting with the daycare director.

At first, we all figured someone was in trouble — maybe we failed to send back a hat with mittens — she was crazy enough to lose her shit over something like that. Turned out it was to make the daycare aware they were separating. A trial separation, as Mrs. Weller said pointedly, according to Traci, our director. Mrs. Type A also clarified she didn't want the staff discussing her or their personal business and that everyone was to act normal. Traci said Jack sat quiet throughout the whole awkward speech, with no opportunity to ask questions or make comments. They were in and out in under fifteen minutes, neither seeing their daughter or taking her with them.

Jack picked her up later that day, last to arrive and looking like hell. As fate would have it, I was closing along with Traci. While Macy played on the swing set, Jack unburdened himself. Like any girl would, I fell head over heels in an infatuation with him. Please, classic chick stuff. Cute, sad guy, all he needs is a little kindness, blah blah blah.

So, long story short, this turns into a not-so-subtle flirtation that goes on for several months. The soon to be ex-wife finds out and I get the evil eye for a while. I bet she was waiting for me to screw up, so she could go off, but she also had to save face. Nothing ever came of anything, and in the meantime, I met Bradley, my future husband and father of my daughter.

Back in those early days, I considered it fun to make Bradley jealous, so I told him about Jack. I liked his reaction, frankly. That's what teenage girls do. It was a mistake. He brought up Jack Weller's name — well, his nick-name — for months.

I had to stop going to that quaint little quirky bookstore on Maple I loved so much, because Jack worked their part time, and there was no way Brad was having any of that. My 'little bookstore boyfriend' he called him, ignoring the fact the Jack Weller towered over him. I had practically lived in that bookstore, and I gave it up without even so much as a goodbye to Rosie, the almost ever-present and eccentric owner. I stopped trying to make him jealous after that. Bradley Handler needed no encouragement anyhow.

Five years. It's so weird to live in the same town with someone — a relatively small town, too — and not see that someone ever. We have two main grocery stores, a

Target, a Wal-Mart, Toys R Us, and lots of little mom and pop run stores. That was kind of it. Just enough civilization to make us modern, balanced out by a quaint hick town feel. How do you not run into people? Mary runs into people all the time, everywhere she goes. Jan, too. Karla? Who knows?

Despite myself, I ask, "Did he move out of town and come back again, or something?"

Mary's eyebrows furrow, "Who? Oh, Jack? No, he's been around. I see him all over the place. I saw him last Thursday at the band fundraiser. Actually, I'm the one that told him about the garden. Said it was only us four and we could use some help, and here he is."

Of course, she did. Mary has three daughters. The twins, Kelsey and Claire were Kadee's age, and her oldest, Holly, was enrolled in at least half a dozen after-school activities, all of which Mary is a volunteer at. Always the social butterfly, she knows just about everyone it seems.

"Wait. So, you told him specifically who would be here?"

Jan cuts in, "I will go with *yes*. Hot daycare dad had the four-one-one you'd would be here, and that's why he suddenly had an interest in digging a stupid fucking community garden that no one will use."

I love Jan's bluntness. But now I'm even more uncomfortable. And a little intrigued. So, because I can't help myself, I glance over at him. A quick side glance. I do it super-fast, but not so fast I don't see him give an awkward half-wave, because he's caught my peep. Fuck.

Fucking, fuck, fuck. Now what? Now I feel like a dick. What the hell do I do now?

God damn it. I give up. He's about three feet away from me, so I can't ignore him anymore.

"Jack? Jack Weller, right? Hey, um, sorry about that. I was, I... So, how've you been?"

Jesus, that wasn't awkward at all. As I walk towards him, brushing dirt onto my baggy cargo shorts and swiping the damp hair off my forehead, I hear Jan not-so-quietly mutter in a singsong falsetto behind me, "Trouble. I smell trouble."

I shoot her a 'shut up' glare, and next thing I know, I'm face to face with Jack fricking Weller. Technically, I'm face to chest with Jack Weller, I'd forgotten how tall he was. Six-foot-three, to be exact. I knew this because I'd asked him all those years ago, standing next to him (too close) on the playground. To my five-foot-two, he was a giant. It's true, everyone is tall next to me, hell even Bradley is.

I distinctly remember wishing he were taller when we dated, but Brad's personality was huge. I've always had a thing for tall guys, so it's kind of ironic that I ended up with an average height Bradley instead.

Anyhow, I am face to chest with Jack Weller. I go to shake his hand, and he comes in for a hug, so it's all incredibly uncomfortable and stupid looking. We both laugh, but I also instinctively scan the street and the parking lot. I feel like Brad's lurking out there, watching.

I always feel like that. When the burly teen boy bagging my groceries offers to load the car I can hear his voice, *'Oh, you'd like that, wouldn't you? You think you're a MILF, now?'* Or the gas station clerk comes out and pumps my gas even though it's self-serve, *'Yeah, sure, he does that for everyone. I'll kick his ass, that fucker.'*

And now. Although this moment is only different in that it's worse. Jack Weller is not a random stranger, he's a part of history. It doesn't matter it's rated PG history.

It still counts in good old bat-shit jealous Bradley World, doesn't it, Brad?

Jack, to my horror, reaches down and wipes away a smudge of dirt from my forehead. The second his fingertips touch my skin, I panic. I guess it's in my eyes. I'll bet I looked like a cornered rabbit right then, based on Jack Weller's worried and apologetic expression. Is it weird that I could feel my pupils dilate, becoming little pinpricks? I swear, it's true. My heart does that elevator drop thing. My peripheral vision goes dark for a second or two. I fucking hate that look. That fucking feeling. He does that to me, Bradley fucking Handler. Even when I don't do a damn thing wrong, even when he is nowhere near me, he fucking does that to me.

My exhale is sharp and I laugh off his concern. I chatter, I realize I'm talking fast, not giving him much chance to answer, let alone ask questions. Karla saves me, asking for help with the 'rake-y thing.' I could hug her, but instead I give Jack Weller an apologetic shrug and walk away. But not before we have what can only be described as 'A Moment.' Jack was a sensitive, intuitive guy. I remember that about him. He could read people, he is reading me. I don't know how I feel about that, but I am sure I like it. And that is a problem. We finish up, a full hour before I told Brad we would. I don't text or call to check in, neither does he. I'm both relieved and suspicious.

Mary says, as predicted, "Plenty of time for some wine, right, ladies?"

She looks at me, though, when she says it. She knows what he's like. I guess everyone does, but she stays silent. I give her that face, that grateful, I know you understand, but we're not gonna talk about it, look, and say, "Always time for wine. Let's roll."

Jan huffs, "Oh, my fricking God. Oh, yeah, sorry, Barb. We *always* go to your house. Why don't we do something different? Let's go to Micky's."

I ask, "The sports bar?"

Jan rolls her eyes, "No, Disney World. Yes, the bar."

Karla shrugs, "Oh, either is fine by me."

Mary pouts, "What's wrong with my house?"

Jan sighs dramatically, and cajoles, "Oh, Jesus, Mary — sorry Barb — nothing. I love your house. But I'm single, remember? I would like to venture out in the world. Even if it is on a Saturday afternoon."

Then, across the lot, she shouts, "Hey. Weller. And you... what's her name, Barb?"

"It's Laurie. Must you yell like that," Barb admonishes.

Jan ignores Barb and yells, "Oh, Laurie. Join us. We're going to Mickey's for a drink." Then, in a normal voice, "You, too Barb. Don't act like you don't drink, I know you do."

Oh my God. Seriously?

I give Jan the 'Are you fucking kidding me' glare.

"What? Oh, don't get your panties in a bunch. It'll be fine. And, it'll give us something nice to stare at."

Across the lot Jack Weller is looking at me for a sign whether to accept or decline, and God help me and my better judgment, I shrug. The only one that declines is Laurie Scott, looking a little disappointed that we didn't push her to go. To all our surprise, Barb agrees to join us. So, we pile into Mary's Suburban, Barb and Jack Weller each take their own cars. Less than ten minutes later, we all walk into the sports bar, a motley crew that looks pretty much like everyone else in there on a Saturday afternoon. And I'm thinking, *what the fuck am I doing*?

The saving grace is that Bradley doesn't actually have any friends, not anymore, at least. They all faded away and moved on in different directions. It was no surprise that Sarah, my best friend and Maid of Honor, was first to fade away. Dan Bannett was a close second. After the night we fought about him, we started to only see him occasionally, then almost not at all, until at last, never. Except there was that one last time, about a year ago.

We ran into him at a fancy restaurant in Westdale. Alejandro's on the River, home of overpriced food, snooty wait staff, and a freezing cold dining room. At least for me, it was. But I was also quite anemic and not good about taking those iron pills Dr. Patel insisted I take.

Anyhow, he came up to our table and yelled, "Brad? Bradley Handler, is that you? My God man, I barely recognized you."

Brad stood up, I heard him mutter *fuck* right before turning on the old not so charming Bradley Handler charm, "Dan fucking Bannett, you old son of a bitch. How the hell are you? You remember — "

But before he could re-introduce me, Dan cut him off, "Well, I'll be God-damned. Hey, there little Livvy. Don't tell me you're still with this ugly fuck. Haha. What have you been feeding this guy, huh?. Buddy leave a little for her. Am I right?"

By then, half of the small restaurant's patrons had turned to gawk. The two of them were so loud. They mortified me, but Dan's wife, a round-faced Asian girl who looked only twenty, was unfazed. She studied her nail polish in that bored, I-don't-give-a-fuck way some women have an innate knack for, so I didn't even have someone to commiserate with.

Somehow, we got through what felt like an eternity, even ending up having a drink with them at the bar at the end of the night. Not because we wanted to, but because Dan insisted. Our barely tolerable night was in full-blown ruin. One I heard about and felt the repercussions of for almost two weeks after.

The stupid thing was, Dan looked no better than Brad did. Puffy and balding, a paunch that hung over his brown leather belt, and not even remotely good looking anymore. That was Dan Bannett of today. But still he dwelled on it after, on every detail, real and imagined.

"Did you notice how long Dan stared at your legs?"

I chose not to respond.

"Next time don't wear such a short fucking dress. Or do you like that kind of attention?"

I didn't bother reminding him he bought the damn dress for me. Picked it out himself. Or that Dan was too busy mauling his mail-order bride to pay any attention to me. I let him bitch about everything until he ran out of steam. It felt like forever that car ride.

FOUR *CORNER BOOTHS ARE BEST*

3:52 P.M.

Jan wants to sit by the window, the brightest spot in the room. I lead us, despite her protests, to the farthest nook. I take the corner seat, expecting Mary to follow on one side, Jan on the other. Instead, Mary stops to say hello to a couple at the bar, Barb excuses herself to the lady's room, Karla has to run back to the car. She left her glasses on the seat, and Jan insists that she needs to be on the outside of the table, so she can get up and go for a smoke without having to maneuver around everyone. That leaves

Jack Weller standing uncertainly and scratching the back of his head.

Jan snaps, "Sit, sit. She won't bite for Christ's sake."

His shrug comes across as apologetic. These shrugs. They are like a *thing*. They say, '*I don't know what to say or do here'* and have become our means of interaction. I shrug back. At least he understands the art of unspoken communication. Not like Bradley. No matter what look I give him — whether it's 'Oh, my God, stop talking' or 'Will you please stop doing that in public — he always, *always* shouts, "*What*? What is that face? Fucking say something if you got something to say."

So, here I am, in a table in the corner of Micky's Sports Bar with Jack fricking Weller, looking to the casual observer like any random couple at a bar. For the millionth time, I imagine my husband showing up. It's so real that when the next person who walks into the bar — a short, portly man wearing a red baseball cap — a color Bradley doesn't even own, I am so certain it's him; I shake. The color drains from my face. Jack sees it, *feels* it. Under the table, he puts his hand on my elbow and squeezes. Once. It clears my vision; I realize it's not Brad. It's not.

He is home with Kadee, feeding her a healthy afternoon snack rather than cookies I specifically asked him not to give her. I hope. He's watching the clock the whole time, too. By my watch, I still have an hour, perhaps a little more if I want to risk being late. I can excuse it easily enough. He'll only stay mad long enough to make his point and then he'll tell me — using a not subtle innuendo — I could *make it up to him. Plus*, he'll no doubt add, *you owe me for letting you go out all day.* How do I have this clairvoyance, you wonder? Because we're approaching the evening of a Saturday night and Bradley will have expectations. He always does.

That's Brad's game, and my price for being 'allowed' to do things, *have* things... for a little 'something' in return. Need new clothes? *Sure*, he'll say, *if you blow me. You want to go to the movies with Jan and the girls? That's fine. But. What about what* I *want, Liv?* What is it he's so fond of saying? Oh, yes. *Gotta do your wifely duty first, Liv.*

It isn't until I shudder that I realize Jack Weller's gentle grip is still hot on my elbow. Neither of us has pulled away. Everyone comes to the table from different directions. Barb bustles around with bird-like, purposeful movement, fusses with her blouse, and glances about the room. I'm guessing she now realizes proper Pastor Ted might not approve of their choice in venue. Mary is still talking to the bar side couple, even as she walks away from them and towards our table. Jan had grabbed menus from the next table over and was also returning. Karla has found her glasses. They were on top of her head.

Me? Well, I sit here with this paralyzed too-bright smile plastered on my face, watching them converge and feeling Jack Weller's hand on my arm and his eyes on me. I can't turn and look at him. I can't pull my arm away. I'm sitting beside a handsome, manly smelling man, and picturing Bradley's fleshy, pouty face waiting at home for me, and I want to scream. I just want to fucking scream. So, I do. In my head. Not out loud. Never out loud. Making scenes is Brad's deal, not mine.

No, what the well-behaved Olivia Handler does is reach up and take the outstretched menu, letting my elbow slipping out of Jack Weller's grasp with a mix of relief and disappointment. The spot where his hand had rested feels cool, damp. I have an urge to check for a damning handprint on my skin, a telltale of my betrayal.

My nerves are causing involuntary waves of body tremors. It's that, and not the weak AC blowing the stale air around. Barb sees one of my teeth-chattering shakes.

"Oh, Livvy dear, are you cold? I have a cardigan in the car..."

Jan scoffs, "How can you be cold? It's an oven in here."

Karla frets, "There's a bug going around, you know. Oh, I hope you're not sick." She pulls her hand sanitizer from her enormous purse.

Jack Weller, in his smooth, low voice says, "Jan? It's Jan, right? See if the waitress can bring water." He says, "You're dehydrated, sweetheart. Let's get you some water, hmm?"

And the way Jack Weller looks at me — the way they *all* study at me in that moment — I almost open the flood gates. Almost. But then the waitress arrives. She's super cheerful, considering it's a sweltering Saturday afternoon in a bar with dim lighting and about a dozen day drinkers, including us six. She's so chipper she takes all the attention off me and I'm thankful for the small distraction. All but Jack Weller's. I can't figure out what to do with his attention, or with my feelings at the moment, so I pretend I'm engrossed in chipper Honor — really, that's her name, says so on her plastic name tag — and her recitation of today's martini specials. Jack Weller interrupts Honor to ask for a glass of water, he hasn't forgotten. He wouldn't.

Happy bouncy Honor lets out an eardrum piercing squeal, in which the elongated words *'Mister Weller'* can sort of be deciphered. At this obvious recognition, he blushes and hand motions for her to hush. But he's smiling. Enjoying the attention of this girl young enough to be his daughter.

I'm a little pissed, on a couple levels. One, that God damn squeal turned every head in the bar on our table. Two, I think I'm jealous. Like I've a right or reason to be. That pisses me off, too.

Before the squeal even tapers off, the physical assault on my personal space begins. I'm getting sandwiched between Honor and awkward but pleased Jack Weller, because she has decided she *must* hug Mister Weller no matter how inconvenient said hug is for me, the person who's inhaling her apple-scented shampoo and whose throat is being compressed by Honor's jutting elbow.

She uses my knee and shoulder to right herself again, and explains with giddy excitement, "Oh, my God, la-*dies*. Mr. Weller is the bestest, ever. I practically grew up at your house, right, Mr. Weller? Brittany — that's Mr. W's oldest daughter — and I were like, in-SEP-ra-ble in high school. Am I right?"

Jack Weller chuckles, "You are right, indeed, Honor. How are you these days? Have you seen Brittany since she's been on break?"

Honor bobs her perfect pony-tailed head, "Oh, totally. We hung out last night over at Mrs. Wel— at Britt's mom's, then went out for sushi, and then like, dancing, and well, you know."

Ah, the infamous ex-Mrs. Weller, twice removed. Or once removed? Whatever. Everyone smiles with polite expectance at Honor, who after a pause, comes to.

"Water. Right. Coming right up. Gosh, it's so good to see you Mr. Weller. Um, so I'll go get that water, and when I get back, I'll take your orders."

I'm serious, everything she says ends in a virtual exclamation points. She is quick with the water, thankfully, and also with a round of drinks. And then the second. And then the third. During the second round, I feel my cell phone vibrate. Once, twice, silent. It was a text, Brad, no doubt. I turn away towards the corner and pull out my phone from my purse.

how much longer. we

hungry. K wants you.

He's sent the same message four times, one minute apart. And will keep sending it till he gets the answer he wants. But the alcohol is making me feel defiant. I answer back.

Soon. Leftover chicken
In fridge. Heat for one
minute. Tell K mom
home soon. Plz.

What he'll actually say to Kadee is, *Well, Kadee, Mommy is out having too much fun with her friends to take care of us, so looks like Daddy has to do everything.* Then he'll give her Goldfish and chocolate milk and will eat a quart of ice cream straight from the carton while Kadee trashes her playroom because he's planted in front of the television. My phone vibrates again.

hurry up

Bradley sends this text eleven times, in two-minute intervals. I ignore all but the last one when I am so fucking pissed off and embarrassed because everyone can tell that my phone is blowing up. I excuse myself and go outside the bar's side door, to the designated smoking area/patio. There's one old guy out there, sitting on a plastic chair, feet propped on the railing, blowing smoke up into the spring sky and ignoring me.

Good. No, forget that. I don't fucking care. When you're a one drink girl, two and a half will do that to you. I'm feeling pretty fucking feisty right now, so I call him. As I stare over the tree line at the distant menacing clouds, I take a deep breath and start in on him the second he answers.

"Bradley, what the fuck? I said I will be home soon."

"Why aren't you home now? How much fucking dirt can you dig?"

"We are at..." I almost lie and say we're at Mary's house. But he'll check with Bob, Mary's husband, and will do it in his sneaky way. "Micky's. Barb wanted to take us out for a drink to say thanks, and I couldn't refuse."

"Well, that's really fucking nice. Kadee and I are home starving, and you're out drinking with your girlfriends. At a bar. Are there guys there?"

"Jesus Christ, Bradley. It *is* a bar, yes there are guys here. No, no one is talking to me."

"Uhh-huh. Bunch of chicks in a bar, and no guy is hitting on you? Yeah, right. What, are they *just being nice*? Jesus, you are so dumb. Don't make me come down there."

"Bradley, so help me God. *Please* do not embarrass me and come down here. I will fu— "

I stop myself. This is what he wants, for me to lose it. Deep breath. "I will be home soon, but I can't leave because Mary drove us."

"I thought you said Barb took you out? Now it's Mary? Make up your mind, Liv. See, that's what happens when you lie."

"Holy fucking-shit, Brad. I'm *not* lying. I am here with MARY, JAN, BARB and KARLA. To-geth-er. Mary drove us in her car, Barb took her own because she lives on the other side of town."

"Why are you getting so mad? I'm just asking you a question."

Again, he fucking does this. That roller coaster of anger, guilt, petulance. I swear a couple times, tell him I'll text when I'm on my way, and hang up. An ocean wave of panic churns and surges in my stomach. It's the Jesus-fucking-Christ, this is my life realization, and now I'm close to hyperventilating, but I hang tough till the old guy passes me to go back into the bar. He eyes me, considering whether he should check if I'm okay. I'm sure he heard the whole thing. At least my end. But I don't make eye contact, and it's enough to discourage him.

The second I hear the soft click of the door behind him, I lose it. Quietly, though. I was raised to keep my shit together. At the farthest part of the makeshift deck, I grip the railing, hard. The wood digs into the thin flesh of my palms, the sting of my new blisters, and I don't fucking care. It's distracting me from crying, I can focus on my breathing.

I'm still gulping air, but it's getting better. Please don't let anyone come out here I say in my head repeatedly. No one can see me like this. Despite my best effort, one fucking tear sneaks it way out, but it's only me out here, so it's okay.

I hear the door click, a creak, then click again behind me.

Please let it be the old guy again. Make him a chain smoker. C'mon, c'mon. Be the old guy.

But I already sense it's not. I understand without turning around that it is Jack Weller come to find me. How could I know this? Because that's the kind of shit that happens in movies and in books, and my life is playing out exactly like something pulled from fiction.

The gravel crunches under his feet as he approaches, and then his tanned, sinewy hand is beside mine on the railing. Jack Weller is beside me, and Brad? Well, he's behind every bush and every corner, up on the roof, behind the dumpster. He's fucking everywhere. I'm not the lion pacing the cage right now. I'm the rabbit in the trap.

But who's the hunter? Bradley? Or is it Jack fricking Weller, showing up out of the blue, right when I'm on the verge of... of what? A nervous breakdown? What am I on the verge of? Running?

I think about that — running — every day. Putting Kadee in the car and just... drive. And drive, and drive and drive. Right to the farthest part of the universe.

Change our names, dye our hair. The physical urge is so strong. Left onto the highway on-ramp instead of straight. Drive, and drive, and drive until the sun goes down and up again. Find a small town, even smaller than this one. A town like in Murphy's Romance, that old Sally Field and James Garner movie I loved. A dream, that's what that is. Just a damn dream.

It would shock Brad if he knew. Shock and scare him, and furious. And I don't even realize I'm doing it, but somehow, I am saying this to Jack Weller. All of it. Out in the open. All those words I never say, they are said. I'm afraid to look at him, afraid I'll see shock and disgust in his eyes. What kind of woman thinks like that? I say this out loud, too. I tell silently listening Jack Weller, "It's not like he's abusive, for God's sake. He's not. He is vulgar and yes, demeaning, but he's never raised a hand to me, honest. I want for nothing, Jack. Nothing. New clothes? Sure. Stay home and raise Kadee? Okay. Plant a garden, paint the living room, whatever I want. The man loves me. I really believe that. Despite how he talks. He's insecure, you know? That's why he acts the way he does. So, I think I'm a really, really shitty, ungrateful person, you see? Why can't I be fucking happy with what is, Jack?"

Jack sighs next to me. It's a sad sound. He's sad for me.

"Oh, little Livvy. You were so full of life back in the day care center days. Christ, you were a kid yourself, really. I had no business flirting with you back then, God knows. Jesus. I was a father, *am* a father. But, God. If you could've seen yourself through my eyes... you were magical. You wanted to be an actress, I recall. You were going to devour the world. Where did you go, Livvy?"

He says it the same way I ask myself, in my head. And it breaks me. I shake my head. I'm embarrassed and don't even know how to answer that question. It's too deep a question; he understands that I've lost me, the 'me' I was supposed to be. Bradley took that from me, but only because I let him.

I *let* him steal me, and now he owns me like a car and a house and the '67 Mustang collecting dust in the garage. Livvy Handler, property of Bradley Handler. I let myself become *property*. The fighting, resisting day in and day out, it became too much, and I threw in the towel, waved the white flag, and let Brad win. And, yeah, I'll admit it. I liked — I *like* — the pretty package with the shiny bow that is my life. I just don't like the hands holding the box.

Jack Weller places a tentative, gentle hand around my upper arm. The first gentle touch from a man's hand in over four years. So, I let him turn me towards him. I'm afraid he'll kiss me, and more afraid I might not stop him if he does. The martinis. The damn martinis, I blame them, but that's not it. They're an excuse. But Jack Weller does not kiss me, he instead does something way more intimate; he embraces me. My cheek is against the softest cotton shirt I've ever felt. Brad's are always rough and stiff But Jack? He smells like a mixture of fabric softener, deodorant and cologne.

Jack Weller has one hand at the back of my head, massaging my scalp through my thick hair, his other arm wrapped around me. And I am letting him. I'm allowing this strange and familiar man hug me. I'm not hugging him back though. I tuck my arms in between us — the brushed cotton fabric of his shirt crumpled in my clenched fist — that's how I rationalize this to myself, to Bradley, as if he were here. But I am letting him wrap his amazing smelling body against me, my head is against his broad chest, for this one moment in time, because I need this. I need it so fucking bad.

Behind us, the door clicks. I jump two feet away from Jack Weller, heart racing and guilty looking. Jack Weller looks calm, in control. Except he's not calm. I could feel as much in that hug, behind the zipper of those khaki shorts pressed up against my waist. There's a perverse glee I feel at that knowledge, and it confirms to me I'm a shitty human. I deserve someone like Bradley Handler. Not this handsome, gentle sweet man.

Jan says, "Ah. Here you two are. You're killin' me here. Mary keeps talking about the spots on her glass, Karla is asking for someone to turn the karaoke machine on. Oh, and Barb's trying to get me to join First Congregational. Save me."

She's playing it cool in front of him, but I'll get grilled later. I follow Jack Weller, who's already walking in ahead of me, and Jan holds me back with a very transparent,

"Stay with me while I have a smoke. You go ahead and handle those crazy broads for me, will you Jack, buddy? There's a good boy."

So, I guess later is right now. The second the door clicks shut, Jan starts, "And what was that all about? You two looked like you got caught with your hands in the cookie jar."

She didn't see the hug. Jan would never pretend she didn't, it's not in her DNA. I struggle with what to tell her. It's the worst-kept secret what a possessive asshole Brad is. They all know. But for my own sanity, I *have* to act like it doesn't bother me, make excuses for his behavior and the obnoxious way he orders me around in front of them. I need to save some sense of dignity. *He* believes he's being funny, showing off for the adoring crowd. But they think he's a dick and they tolerate him for my sake. And worse, they pity me. I can see it in their eyes.

Mary's husband Bob almost clocked Brad once at a party. Brad was oblivious. But I wasn't. I saw Mary grab his arm, plead with her eyes to let it go. I've known Bob for as long as I've known Mary. They were high school sweethearts who got married right out of college. He's always treated me like a kid sister.

When Bradley went to use the bathroom — mercifully and unwittingly breaking the building tension — I followed Bob into the kitchen under the guise of getting ice. But I wanted to thank him and apologize once again for Brad's behavior.

I gave him a quick, awkward side hug as he emptied the trash. He was still trying to calm down and couldn't stay silent like Mary had begged. "Liv, kiddo, what the fuck is wrong with that guy, man? He can't just talk to you like that. I'm tryin' here, but he doesn't fucking quit. Is he hitting you? You tell me right now, is he hitting you?"

As touched as I was for his concern, I was also embarrassed and humiliated that my friends suspect he hits me, that I'd let him do that. That I'm that weak. No.

"He's never raised a hand to me," I told Bob. His eyes searched mine for a moment, then he nodded.

I'll say this, because it's true. If Bradley ever did lay a hand on me, I'd kill him. I swear to God, I'd kill him with my bare hands. Deep down, he knows it, too. Really deep down, Brad's afraid of me. Okay, afraid of *losing* me, is more like it. He wouldn't risk it. So, I let Bob know I'm fine, I can handle Brad Handler and please don't worry. And it's true, I can. I've been handling him for over four years now, and it's down to a fucking science.

So, yes. Jan knows a lot. More than what she lets on, and even still, she says more than most people would. My own family says less than she does. Even though I could tell her everything, I hold back. I hold it in because that's what I do. That's what's in *my* DNA. A steadfast habit of repression and suppression. A virtual brick wall of self-imposed isolation. I can probably thank my upbringing for that as much as I can thank Bradley. They taught me how to stack those bricks. My grandma was fond of saying that it didn't matter if World War III was happening in your home, the minute that doorbell rings, you put on your face and smile. Period. That's what we call in my family, 'putting on your face.' Bradley taught me how to mortar them good and thick.

So, out of habit more than necessity, I put on my face for Jan, and even though I could see she didn't buy it, not one bit, I smiled and said, "No, silly. He just happened to come out while I was talking to Bradley, and well typical me, I get so awkward. Poor guy was just being nice. Now stop giving me that face. Let's go back inside."

I give her no opportunity to rebut, linking my arm through hers and pull her through the door as she flings her half-smoked cigarette behind her. We walk in to the sounds of Barb, Mary and Karla warbling 'I Will Survive' into a single microphone. A fourth round of drinks sits on the table, along with four empty shot glasses. I look at Jan with raised eyebrows.

"Oh, yeah, we may have had a round of shots while you two were out there making googly eyes at each other."

I physically recoil, shocked she would say that out loud. Oh, my God, were we that obvious? Was *I* that obvious? Nervously I glance around the room. The sparse crowd that was here when we arrived has now doubled. It seems like all eyes are on me even though they are not. But still. I feel that panicky sensation creeping up again and realize they are all too drunk to get me back to my car before Bradley starts a full-on shit fit.

Without even looking, I can guess he has texted me at least twice more. I have to get the fuck out of here. Something presses against my arm. It's my purse. Jack Weller is pressing my purse into my hands and guiding me back out the side door by my elbow without a word. I'm too startled to resist. No one seems to notice, including Jan, who is now singing with the others.

Behind me — *Jack Weller* and me — the metal utility door clicks once again and the unmistakable smell of rain on the horizon replaces the loud bar music and stale beer smell. The world has taken on that eerie green hue that comes right before a doozy of a storm. I feel that balloon feeling again. Like I'm floating up and away from the earth, but Jack Weller's deep voice grounds me in an instant.

"Wait here."

Then he dashes off around the side to the front of the building. He'll get his car and bring it around back where I stand in a trance. He expects me to leave with him. Alone. In his car. Has he gone mad? Have I? I may have, because God help me, I will get in his car when it rolls over the gravel beside this poor excuse of a deck.

FIVE *THE SKY OPENS*

5:10 P.M.

The car does pull up, a white boxy looking SUV with tinted windows and an OBX decal on the back window and a roof rack on top. I take one step, then hesitate. His window glides down halfway and our eyes lock. His expression is unreadable. He is simply waiting, trying not to influence me either way. But he's hoping I'll jump in the passenger side.

The sky decides for me, or at least I let that be my reason. Fat drops of rain splat on the deck, resin tables and cheap plastic chairs like June bugs hitting a windshield. Holding my purse over my head, I run around the front of Jack Weller's SUV and slide into the passenger seat, slamming the door behind me. The AC is on, freezing on my wet skin and I shiver. Jack turns down the air, rolls up his window and puts the car in drive. We don't say a word. Bob Seger sings softly from the speakers.

Now the raindrops that had started off slow and fat are bucketful waves of torrential downpours. The five-fifteen p.m. sky looks more like nine p.m. as we pull out of the lot, turning slowly onto Beecher Street, towards Main, towards the darkest part of the sky. Jack Weller is driving slow, headlights on and windshield wipers beating fast and hard, like my heart.

I feel... I feel anonymous. So, I settle back into the tan leather seat, conscious of the goosebumps on my arms and the nearness of Jack Weller. I smell his scent stronger in here. That smell will be on me when I get home, and if Brad gets close enough to smell it, he will lose his mind. I'll figure that part out later. Right now, I feel deliciously reckless. I'm pretending I am free, like I'm Jan and I don't give a shit.

"Livvy. I want to see you. Again, I mean. Would that be all right?"

Jack Weller's earnest sexy voice breaks the spell. Just like that, I crash back to reality. *See* me? I'm married. To a jealous psycho. Fine, he's not a full-blown psycho, but I've always made sure to not give him a reason to be. Until now.

"Jack, I—"

"It's okay, Livvy. I understand. I — I want you to understand that. Nothing will happen here. I know that, too. But it's not because I don't want it to. I respect you, Liv. And I don't believe you're a shitty person, by the way. You're a beautiful young woman who still has the world open to her... and who is afraid."

What can I say to that? Nothing. I say nothing, because I the sting of tears prickles my eyes, and I can't. So, I nod. In another universe, I'd so love to see Jack Weller again. Date. Talk about life, dreams, anything. I'm not that seventeen-year-old, inexperienced girl anymore. I'm a woman in a car with a sexy man, and I want to disappear with him, if only for a little while.

Instead, I'll be going home to the vile human I married soon because I see now that Jack Weller is bringing me to the church parking lot, where both mine and Jan's cars are getting battered by the hard rain. I'm disappointed and relieved. And something else. Tired. I'm so fucking tired.

As Jack Weller backs into the space next to Jan's car (not mine, thank God. He's got the good sense to not park next to mine) I turn and study him for the first time. I decide I love the scruff along his solid jaw-line and creeping up his cheek to a neat angled line. His nose isn't perfect from the front (broken twice while playing hockey in his teens) but from the side, it's nice. The faint lines at the corners of his eyes. I remember those from back in the hot day care dad days. They have deepened, but it only makes him sexier. He's rugged. Manly. Yet when I gaze into them, I see he's careworn. He kind of looks like that guy that some ocean show that Brad's always watching. There's a gentleness to him. Perhaps raising three daughters will do that to a man, but God knows raising one hasn't changed Brad. I will not think of *him* and his crude and vulgar mouth while I sit next to this perfect specimen of a man who looks like a guy on television.

"I'd forgotten how much I liked you, Jack Weller. How much I like saying your name. Jack Weller. You're like a character out of all those books you were always recommending."

He chuckles low; I can feel it vibrate against my back in the leather seat. "You remember that, do you? Ahh, little Livvy, I remember a lot of things too. Like the last time I saw you."

He's parked the car, turned the headlights off, stopped the wipers and lowered the music even more. I can still make out the sounds of Lindsay Buckingham's guitar playing the familiar chords to 'Bleed to Love Her.' One of my favorite songs, but not one that gets much radio play, not even on the 'classic rock' stations. I glance down at the dash and see it's a CD. Surprised, my head jerks up at Jack Weller. He nods.

"Is that...?" I trail off.

He knows what I'm asking. He shrugs, nods again, begins to say something, changes his mind, and then gives in, "Livvy, I was crazy about you. Like a God-damn school boy, a too old-to-be-acting-like-a-school-boy grown man, head over heels, crazy. Yes, crazy enough that I still have this CD."

That was my CD. Literally, mine. I'd burned a playlist of all my favorite songs, many of them obscure odd songs out of time for my age and listened to it all the time. Then there was that one day. I was on break and sitting in my car singing along to the music and eating from a box of cereal. Jack Weller snuck up beside my driver's side window, standing there for God knows how long, until I saw him in my side-view mirror and jumped a mile, spilling cereal all over the car and myself.

"Love your music choices, little Livvy," he said.

So, I hit the eject button and handed the CD to him. I acted so fearless back then. Flirting was a sport, and I was all-star material. I actually winked at him when I said, "Take it... so you can think of me when you listen to it."

I remember it clearly, even now. The dogwood tree I'd parked under dropping broad pink petals on my hood. The faint sound of children from inside the building. Jack, gazing down at my upturned face through the open window. He looked like a guy with a school boy crush in that moment. A too-old-to-be-acting-like-a-schoolboy guy with a crush.

He said, "I suspect you might be playing the role of Nabokov's Lolita, little Livvy."

I laughed. I'd never read the book, but I knew the reference thanks to the Police song. "Am I, Mr. Weller?"

He wagged his finger at me, grinning, and said, "Oh, you are trouble, aren't you?"

"Yes, but the best kind."

Jack Weller crouched down, folded his arms on the window ledge, and rested his chin on top. Our faces were inches apart. My heart pounded, but I leaned in. The second before our lips touched, a car door slammed. We jumped away as if stung.

Jack rubbed at the back of his neck and looked sheepish. "That was — I," he stammered, then laughed.

I climbed out of the car, darting glances around the lot. It was a no-brainer that a staff-parent relationship was a no-no. "I've got to get back inside. See you later." I rushed by without looking up at him. The next day I went to the Book Haven and bought the book and read it in one night. It discomfited me, enough, so I began to second-guess our little flirtation. I was seventeen. What was he? Forty? Close to it at least.

As if reading my mind, "I was forty-one, Livvy. No business flirting with you. None. I don't know, I just — "

"Jack don't beat yourself up. It was mutual. Hell, I provoked you, encouraged you. I was a little crazy about you, myself. I was a wild kid back then. Hard to imagine now, isn't it?" Wry chuckle.

Jack smiled, but it didn't reach his eyes. "But then you pulled away. That last time I saw you — in the bookstore, you walked in, headed straight for your favorite section. I watched you pick up each book and put them back until you found your favorite. The Complete C. S. Lewis, leather-bound limited edition. You walked towards the register with it clutched to your chest like someone would steal it from you. When you looked up and saw me, you froze. I was smiling like a fool, and you turned your head to the door — at the guy who was there — his arms across his chest and looking out of place in a bookstore. And pissed. Then you set the book down on the table next to you, like you're putting down a baby, and walk out the door without a second glance. Gone, Livvy, gone. Never to be seen again."

"Until now," I whisper.

"Yes, until now. I always wondered what happened. But now I understand. That was him, Livvy, your husband, wasn't it?"

My sigh is heavy and there's a shakiness to it I don't like. Yes, I tell him. That was him. I remember that day, too. I'd wanted that book forever. It was a collector's special edition, $89.99, leather bound, all the works of C.

S. Lewis in one book, including copies of hand-written notes and pictures by and of the author. I could never justify spending the money on it.

I have no idea why, but I told Brad about the book, and he wanted to be generous and buy it for me. When we got to the bookstore, I headed straight for the corner it sat waiting for me, exactly like Jack Weller recalled. He stood in the doorway. Brad Handler hated bookstores… and boutiques, and antique stores, libraries, coffee shops. All the places I love.

Brad recognized Jack from the one time he picked me up at work and caught us chatting. Flirting, he called it. Rightly, I suppose. He knew all about Jack Weller, thanks to an immature impulse to him about the 'hot day care dad' and how all the girls were smitten with him. So, when he saw the infamous Jack before I did, his green-eyed monster reared its ugly head.

"When I went in there that day, I had no idea you worked in the bookstore." I sighed, shaking my head at the memory.

"Ah, yes. You remember Rosie, the owner? She's my cousin. I was helping family," he said.

"I froze, Jack. I was so afraid Brad would make a scene. Believe me, he was not above doing that. I put down my precious book as fast as I could and left."

"Liv? What are you doing with this guy? What hold does he have on you? You can't be happy, I know you can't."

"Happy? What's that? I'm kidding, kidding. Listen, I'm... happy, in my way. I have my little girl, Kadee. She's three — turning four in July, actually — and she's the best. I have a pretty house. Garden in the back yard. It's nice. It's a good life, Jack, it is. I can't complain."

"Yes, I get it. You *'don't want for anything.'* Isn't that what you said back there at the bar? What about *love*, Livvy? Tenderness? Understanding? Friendship? What about those things? Do you have those?"

"I guess if you're asking, you've already guessed the answer, haven't you, Jack?"

If I appear half as lost as I feel in this moment, Jack Weller should send out a search team. But as it is, my husband will do exactly that if I'm gone much longer. I don't dare peek at my phone. My only security is that he won't take Kadee out in the rain. Not for any other reason than it's too much work to get her ready and into that car seat he always bitches is too complicated.

"Jesus, Livvy. You can't live like this. It's not right. You deserve to be happy."

"Ah, Jack. What do you know of me, really? *Do* I deserve to be happy? Why? Because you think I'm pretty? What if I'm ugly inside? What if I'm a horrible person?" Since I can't face him, I face the window when I ask, "What if what I deserve is exactly what I've got? They say there's a price for everything in life. I get Kadee, a nice house, everything I could ever want, hell I've almost got him convinced on a dog. My price? Well, I guess my price is an eternity with a vulgar man I hate." When I turn back to Jack, it's with every ounce of despair plain on my face, and I confess. "I hate him, Jack. I really do. How's that for pretty? Still say I deserve to be happy?"

Jack Weller is giving me those sad, sympathetic puppy eyes again. Like he gets it. But he can't, possibly. What he's probably thinking, and hiding well, is that yes, I am in fact a shitty person, and please get the hell out of his car. Which it is more than time to do.

Suddenly claustrophobic, I reach for the door. If I look at that handsome, rugged, and sweet face one more second, I might beg him to take me home with him. He puts his hand on mine. The one not reaching for the door but clutching my purse. I stay for a second longer, suspended at the moment, but I don't turn back.

"Thank you for the ride, Jack. I—I've got to go."

Before he can say another word, I'm running through the pouring rain to my car. I fumble for the keys I'd forgotten to take out before I left the dry safety of his car, and curse as they fall in the crater sized puddle at my feet. I'm digging around in the cold muddy water, crying.

Fucking fuck fucker.

The rain plasters my hair to my head and in my face, tears and rain are all the same. And Jack fucking Weller is right there like a hulky angel, one strong arm around my waist, lifting me away from the puddle and placing me behind him. He reaches into the water and snatches the keys from the miniature pond as if he has x-ray vision.

The next thing I know, his arms wrap tight around me, and though I've buried my face in my hands, I'm pressed against his chest. It is pouring, we're soaked to the bone, and for the first time in four years, I cry. I didn't think I could cry in front of another human being, but I can, and I do.

In the scary safety of Jack Weller's arms, I cry like I've lost the world. He gets me to my car, releases the lock with my remote, and once he's put my seat belt across me, he starts my car. I stare into his wet hair, rivulets dropping onto my lap, and I want to reach up and stroke the dark wet strands, but I keep my hands on my lap. Jack Weller turns his rain-soaked face to mine, and I'm afraid he's going to kiss me. And he does, but on my forehead.

"Go home, little Livvy. Tell him you're sick. Take a bath. Kiss your little girl and go to bed. Tomorrow is a new day."

Before I can answer, he's closed the driver door, and is sprinting back to his car. The rain has slowed. Once he is in his own car, he flicks his headlights once, twice. Telling me to go first, so I do. I pull out of the lot, turn left. In my rearview mirror, I see the white SUV turn left and disappear.

I don't have to pull down the visor mirror to see I'm a mess, but I do it anyway. My eyes go straight to my forehead, where Jack Weller pressed his lips before dashing off, half expecting to see a telltale mark, like his lip-prints or a scarlet letter giving my betrayal away. There's nothing there but a memory.

I almost blow the stop sign but slam my brakes at the last instant. I have this awful split-second hope I'll get into an accident and won't have to face Brad, but I'm alone on the road. Not another car in sight until I reach our street. Phil is backing out of his driveway, next to ours. No doubt running to the store for one of Lisa's pregnancy cravings. I say she's full of shit and likes to see him jump at her every whim. I didn't have that many cravings with Kadee, aside from chocolate peanut butter cups.

One particular night, mid-way through the pregnancy, I said, half joking, I had to have them, or I'd die. To his credit, and that very night, he made sure I got what seemed like a lifetime supply in the spare freezer in the basement. Like everything else he does, Brad went over the top. There is still a case buried under frozen steaks, pork chops, and burgers, probably with freezer burn by now.

He bragged to everyone that *'Livvy just had to have chocolate peanut butter cups,'* so he had to get for me. *'Bought the whole damn town out of the shit, that's what I did,'* he'd bellowed. Then added, *'Because princess gets what princess wants. Isn't that right, Princess?'*

He has told that same story in the same way at least fifty times, and to people who've already heard it. How does he not see that glazed look in their eyes, or notice they finish the sentence for him? How is he not aware of my mortification at that characterization? Me, a princess? A term I once thought sweet and endearing, is repulsive and demeaning from Brad's thin lips and condescending tone.

Whether it's done consciously or not, it is always said in that way so as not to imply a sentiment of reverence and regality, but rather one of spoil and indulgence. I am not that girl.

I'm not, damn you, Bradley.

SIX *HOME DAMN HOME*

6:27 P.M.

I'm in the driveway. A twitching, shaking jumble of nerves. I've come up with four stories, settled on one. Rehearsed it. I've already talked to Bradley in my head, the one I can tell to fuck off with no repercussions. The kitchen light is on as are the playroom and the living room lights. I take a deep breath and another quick peek in the visor mirror, I open the car door and step out into the humid early evening air.

The storm has passed, a late day sun is peeking out behind the last of the clouds and steam is rising off the pavement. I smell the earthy smell I always associate with worms and spring, and the driveway is littered with them. I hate that smell.

When I walk in the back door, I'm reciting my excuses in my head. But then I hear the TV is on loud in the living room and not one, but two voices are shouting at the screen. Baseball and his brother, no doubt with a case of beer for each of them.

My knees buckle with relief. He won't be bothering me tonight, not as much, at least. Not in front of his brother, and not while baseball was on. Kadee must be up in her playroom, so I try to slip past Bradley and Karl with a quick hello, but he stops me.

"Well, well, look what the cat dragged in, Karl. It's Princess Livvy looking like a drowned rat. Nice of you to come home to your family. You remember me, right? The guy who funds all your little escapades?" He rolls his fat head to his brother, and adds, "Swear to God, Karl, if this one could ever earn some money with all that volunteering she does, I'd be rich."

I don't recite for him the definition of a volunteer, but instead say, "Sorry, Bradley. Hi Karl. I'll just go up and see Kadee. How was she?"

Karl raises his beer in salute but doesn't take his eyes off the screen. Typical Karl response.

"I dunno, call my mother and ask her."

"What? What do you mean? She's at your mother's? Why didn't you tell me?"

"Well, if you'd answered my texts, I would have. She came by earlier, asked Kadee if she wanted to stay over Grandma's tonight and packed her a bag and left. Couple hours ago. You know, while you were out partying it up at the bar. Guess she felt bad for her that her mom wasn't around to watch her."

You fucking, fucking asshole. You know I hate when Rita watches Kadee.

By Rita's standards, I don't feed her enough, dress her warm enough, or do anything right in general. I can hear her now, 'Poor little munch, Mommy leaves you here with these boring men? Come on to Grandma Rita and I'll make you some mac n cheese.'

She knows I hate that boxed, processed food, so she'll make it to spite me. It's what the Handler boys grew up on. Everything came from a cardboard box or can or bag. Vegetables? Corn. Fruit? Hostess (or some other snack company) apple pies. Everything that wasn't from a box, can or bag was chicken or steak. Hell, even the potatoes were boxed.

Still, I feel a little relieved, and then guilty for it. I haven't seen Kadee-Bear since this morning, and now I won't see her until tomorrow morning. I don't have it in me to play fake cheerful right now. Karl's presence meant I at least had a few hours of relative peace. Sure, I'll have to feed them and clean up after them, but if I'm lucky, the two of them will get comatose drunk and I'm free until at least tomorrow afternoon. I grin at little, and Brad catches it.

"What the fuck you grinning at? You still drunk?"

"I'm not drunk, Bradley. I didn't get drunk. I was thinking about Jan and Mary sing—"

"Yeah, yeah, stop there. Don't need to hear about those two dipshits. You're messing up the game. Go make us some of those pizza rolls, will ya? Go on, make yourself useful."

"Bradley, do you see that I am soaking wet? Can I go change at least? Jesus."

He gives me that patronizing and blank stare, that 'did you say something, I couldn't hear you' stare. I decide it's easier if I make the fucking pizza rolls. Karl is pretending not to hear any of it. Both our families do that. We all do what's easier. So, I squelch back into the kitchen, toss my purse onto the table, and that's when I notice it, the thing that peaks out from the open outside zipper, my CD from another lifetime. Jack Weller must've slipped it in there when I was being a hot mess. I tuck it back into my bag. If Bradley sees it, he'll be suspicious and ask, *where the hell did that come from.* And for once, he'll be right to be distrustful.

From the living room, he shouts, "Sometime today, Liv." So instead of putting the damn pizza rolls in the toaster so they'll be crispy — like he likes them — I throw them in the microwave for a few minutes. Shivering and rushing just to shut him up, I grab a scalding hot roll out of the damn microwave, so I can toss them in a bowl. Of course, I burn my hand on the hot cheese that farted out of the tiny factory machine pressed seam. I jerked my hand back, dropping it on the tile floor. After I stare at it for a moment, I shrug and place in the bowl and bury it under the others. Fuck him. He'll never know.

I set the bowl between the two men, which they attack like animals, and he says, "Uh, some papers towels, Liv? We're not fricking animals. Jesus. Do I have to tell you how to do everything?"

"Jesus Christ, Bradley, I'm getting pneumonia here."

"Oh, fuck, here we go. Let me guess. Another excuse why we're not gonna do it tonight, right?"

Karl snorts back a laugh but says nothing.

Well, Bradley, tonight we are not going to 'do it' as you say, because you are a repulsive chauvinistic pig who will get shit-housed tonight and become incapable of getting it up. Thank. Fucking. God.

And yes, I again single handedly set women's lib back and get the paper towels from the kitchen, toss the roll in his ample lap, and then finally go upstairs to draw a hot bath. I pass Kadee's playroom and see that it is trashed. Every single toy, game and doll is out. There's a plate with half a cookie on it and a sippy of chocolate milk and crumbs all over the table, as I expected it would be, but still I want to cry. As much as I know I should wait until tomorrow and make Kadee help with cleaning up the mess, I can't muster that much parental discipline.

if they are still downstairs watching the game after my bath, I'll clean it myself. Or at least half way and finish in the morning while Brad is sleeping off his inevitable hangover and Kadee's still at his mother's.

Once in the bathroom, door locked and alone with the small Bluetooth speaker playing that old playlist from my phone, and a glass of wine I'd snuck from the den, I heave a sigh of relief and think, *what the fuck*. What the fuck just happened? Was that real, even? But one glance over at my purse, which I brought into the bathroom with me, and the telltale glint of the iridescent silver plastic disc, is enough to tell me it was no dream or fantasy, I'd been in Jack Wellers arms, not once but twice in under an hour.

Jack Weller's lips had touched my forehead. His hand had been in my hair, hot against my scalp, his body had been pressed against mine, his dick hard against my belly. Oh, my God. That happened. For the first time in years, I feel aroused. Desire — an almost foreign word for so long — now coursed through my body, sending a literal shock wave into my pelvis. It's been so long since I felt that kind of sexual excitement, I'm amazed I'm still capable. I'm alive after what seems like ages. I can't to go back to that living death I've existed in since I finally saw Bradley for how he is, after it was too late.

Thinking of *him* is ruining the moment, so I turn the music up, the same song that had been playing when I got into Jack Weller's SUV. Bob Seger, You'll Accomp'ny Me. I allow myself to fantasize about Jack Weller's body pressed hard against mine, his strong but gentle hand tangled in my hair.

I fantasize about what I wished had happened. Jack Weller pulling my head back slowly with that hand coiled in my hair, bringing his full lips to mine, gently, hesitantly at first. His beard tickling. His tongue flicks inside mouth, and I gasp. I feel him smile, his perfect white teeth against my parted lips, imagine the barely hidden dimples beneath the stubble on his cheeks and feel the pad of his thumb caress the nape of my neck in slow circles. The bath water moves in those same slow circles, ripples crease the surface in a steady rhythm. For the first time in four years, I'm going to come.

"What the fuck's taking you so long in there? Jesus Christ, I gotta whiz and Karl's dropping a heater in the downstairs bathroom. Move it, Liv."

Bradley, you fucking fucker. I swear to God you have some kind of sixth sense. You seek every moment of joy I might have and destroy it like a heat-seeking missile. Only you could cock block a fantasy.

"Hold *on*, Bradley." Then, under my breath, "God damn it."

That's that. I lift the stopper with my toe and drain my wine as the tub drains the water. Turn off the music, dry off and throw my robe on. I still have a chill, maybe I am coming down with something after all. Wouldn't that beat all? In classic obnoxious Bradley fashion, he has taken to knocking on the bathroom door.

Knock. Knock. *Knockknockknock.* Knock. Knock. Kno —

"I'm OUT. What the fuck, Bradley. All yours, I'm going to bed."

The playroom can wait until tomorrow. After I pass him — *Bradley, you smell like a brewery* — I realize I've left my purse in there. I panic needlessly; I'm overreacting. It's just a CD, but my conscious is wreaking havoc. Thankfully, he's in too much of a rush to notice, bothering with neither flushing nor washing his hands.

You're a class act, Bradley. And you wonder why I won't let you near me until after you've showered.

SEVEN *DISTRACTIONS*

6:03 A.M.

I'm staring at cobalt blue vase on my nightstand, listening to Brad snore. It's a tag sale find he thinks is ugly. Not because it *is* ugly, but because it didn't come from a high-end store with a high price tag. It makes me love it more. The old woman who sold it to me said she'd planned to give it to her granddaughter, but she'd turned her nose at it for the same reason Brad did, only new things with price tags had value.

I recall almost offering to fix her granddaughter up with my husband but bit my tongue. Instead, I offered to pay what she asked, and when she offered to take less, I

84

insisted on paying the full price. We both knew it was worth less than she asked for, but she accepted my money.

She asked, "What's a young girl like you want with an old piece of glass?"

I told her the truth even though I felt silly and sentimental. It was the same color as my grandfather's eyes. My Opa, gone two years that day. I felt like he led me there, to that rinky-dink rummage sale on a cul-de-sac I'd never been on before.

I drove Kadee around, trying to get her to fall asleep — she was tough that first year — and I caught the handwritten sign staked into the grass out of the corner of my eye. I don't remember why I stopped, I hadn't gone to a tag sale since I was a girl, when my grandmother, my Oma, used to drag me along, bargaining and haggling for bits of china. That was her thing, Bavarian china.

Even though Opa could afford to buy her whatever she wanted, she liked finding the bargains. A throwback to their poor days in Germany, I suppose. They didn't like haggling with her, showing up at a tag sale in heels and designer clothes, but she ignored their indignant stares and got the price she wanted. Usually.

Opa would smile and laugh when we returned and tell her what a great treasure hunter she was, pinch her cheek and call her *liebchen*. She would swat his hand away, acting annoyed. '*Ach du Lieber,*' she'd exclaim, but I could see her smirking at his back as he walked away whistling a happy tune. I wanted a marriage like theirs, a life like theirs. I half got it right.

Anyhow, I told the old woman that story, and her eyes got a little misty — her cobalt blue eyes — and she said that was why her Richard bought that vase, years ago in a home goods store. They didn't need it, it didn't even match their décor, but Richard said it matched her eyes and therefore, they needed it. I didn't need her to tell me Richard was no more.

This was an estate sale, everything was going, including her. Probably to a home, was my guess. I looked around the yard. No one was there helping her. So, I let Kadee sleep in the car and helped Genevieve for two hours. When Kadee woke up, she played on a blanket and Genevieve and I drank iced tea and exchanged stories.

I never told Bradley that story. He'd have said it was weird to sit with a stranger all day for no reason, and then he'd ask if 'the old bat' gave me anything for my time.

She's an old woman saying goodbye to her whole life, I'd have said. And he'd have shrugged and told me *good job wasting a whole day*. Bradley Handler would never do something for someone for no reason, no gain.

I'm not ready to get up, but if I stay in bed any longer, there's a chance he'll roll over and swing one bloated hairy arm over my waist, and then I'm trapped until he moves again. With that repugnant image stuck in my head, I climb out of bed, breath held and hoping he doesn't feel the mattress shift. He's on his back, sprawled like a beached whale, with one pale leg over the covers, one under. He slept in tighty-whities again, despite my repeatedly asking that he sleep in the pajamas I bought, like a civilized human being.

I grew up in a world where men all wore pajamas. Buttoned down tops and matching pajama pants. On weekends, they came to breakfast still in those elegant sleep clothes, however they did not come down until after they'd brushed their teeth and hair and washed their faces. But my husband? No, he comes down in his underwear, no shirt. Hair in every direction, smelling of sleep sweat and morning breath. Calls me a priss when I complain. Tells me to lighten up. If a man can't be himself in his own home, then where could he be? Besides, he often adds at the end of every argument, whoever pays the bills around here makes the rules. So, he wins, as usual. I say nothing, react as little as possible. I complete my bathroom routine in the main upstairs bathroom, or as we now call it, Kadee's bathroom, so I don't wake him. I've taken to always doing all of my toiletries in there. It's easier.

Plus, he refuses to put a lock on the master bathroom door, and I can't stand his barging in on me anytime he wants. I don't tell him this though. It'll be an argument, so I say I have too much stuff for us to share a bathroom. It's true enough that he doesn't disagree. He hates seeing feminine products, so it's one of the easiest wins I've had in a long time.

Even though I'm exhausted — emotionally drained from the surreal craziness that was the day before — I'm glad to be awake so early. I love this time, dawn before everyone else is awake. Kadee, like her father, has become a weekend late sleeper. Most weekend mornings I have until eight o'clock before those two rumble upstairs.

Today, Kadee is not here and won't be until lunchtime when Brad's parents and brother get here. Nap-time will be put off. An afternoon with Rita. Ugh. It'll be a long day. But two can play at that game. I'll invite my mother. Brad will disappear into the garage with Karl and his dad and leave me with the two hens and Kadee, but it's better than spending the day cooped up with only him.

If it were just the three of us, he'd insist that I put Kadee down for a nap, and suggest that we 'have a nooner,' while she sleeps. Then he'd waggle those sparse eyebrows in what he thinks is a suggestive way and punctuate the 'spontaneous' idea with a visual, hip thrusts and blow job motions. I'd have to come up with excuse one-hundred-and-one as to why we cannot. Same routine, different day. Getting shot down would lead to asking for at least a hand job, a deed I sometimes give in to so he'll shut up, staring at either the ceiling or the wall, depending on what act I've submitted to.

But today, thank God, I'll be spared. I smile as I walk into the sunny kitchen. I'd remembered to set the auto brew on the coffee maker and the heavenly scent filled the room. I take my steaming cup out onto the back porch and sit in the rocker facing the sun and the garden. It's still dew damp, but I don't mind. I'm too busy planning my day. If I time everything right, I'll have the next two hours to play in the garden, an hour and a half to shower, change and prep for company. Perfect.

But right now? Right now, I will drink my coffee, turn my face to back toward the sun, and close my eyes. And breathe. No thinking. No thinking. No... fuck. I'm thinking. More, I'm picturing. Jack Weller's face behind my eyelids. Not an unwelcome vision, but one I must erase. As quickly as possible. Lord knows I thought enough about him during the night.

During that fitful sleep — one punctuated by Brad's stumbling, belching, farting bedroom entrance after 2 A.M., during which I pretended to be deep asleep — I dreamed and fantasied about Jack Weller and this fine mess I've gotten myself into. I recreated the scenes of the day in my head, with alternate endings. Some were nice, others were not. The last one, right before my eyes opened and focused on that cobalt blue vase, was the most pleasant of all. And that was how I knew it was a dream.

I have to stop this. It was a nice, ego boosting moment. Leave it at that and make the best of this life I've chosen. This is my lot. As I take in everything that surrounds me, I remind myself it ain't so bad.

So, quit your bitchin', buck up and shut up. Life is good. Be fucking happy. You dumb fuck, you. That's what I'm telling myself, in Bradley's grating voice. That's my self-pep talk. I just called myself a dumb fuck, exactly like he would. He'd say a lot worse if he had any idea of my thoughts, or the events of yesterday.

A cold spike of fear pierces my stomach. My heart skips with a thud. He will find out. I'm certain he will. Someone must have seen us. I'm not worried about Jan or Mary, and Karla was oblivious. Barb? Barb could be the loose cannon. Wait. We don't go to church. Barb has never even met Bradley. Jesus. I think I need to go to church and confess my sins. Do they do that at First Congregational?

They're Protestant. I think. What do Protestants do?

Fuck it. Drink your coffee, Livvy.

Little Livvy. That's what Jack Weller called me. Even back in the day care days. Fuck. STOP it. Inhale. Exhale. Repeat. Focus on the garden. That's what I'll do. My coffee's gone cold now anyhow, and my nightgown is damp, straight through my robe. I stare down at my watch and am stunned to see it's already eight-fifteen. How did two hours pass by? I run in the kitchen, down to the basement and rummage through the laundry for gardening clothes. Tank top, cargo shorts socks. Boom. Almost the replica of yesterday's outfit, different colors.

I dash up the stairs in my socks and almost break my neck. Last week I yanked the carpeting off the stairs with every intention of replacing it, but I haven't gotten that far. Tomorrow, when Kadee is napping, I'll do it.

I slip my gardening boots on at the back door where they otherwise stay like good little ducks at attention. Brad says they are ugly. I love them. Bright yellow with handles on either side. I think they're lovely. What a surprise. We disagree on something. It's now eight-forty. How does time keep getting away from me?

Three and a half hours later, there are twelve tidy rows of alternating stubby green plants and dirt covered seeded mounds. I haven't looked at the time; I've been lost in a moment, headphones on and my seventies rock playlist in my ears. It isn't until Kadee tackles my knees while Brad and his mother are standing at the back door. Rita is laughing at me, he is glaring. Great.

EIGHT *RITA AND HER SON*

12: 35 P.M.

Brad has just woken up, no doubt thanks to the piercing voice of his mother shouting, '*Helllloooo, anybody home,*' throughout the house. She has an annoying habit of letting herself in. In his usual 'what the fuck' tone, he sneers, "Nice job watching the time, Liv. We're starving."

"Bradley, if you were starving half as much as you always say you are— " Fuck, that was my outside voice. I am slipping.

Brad, baiting, "What's that, Liv? What?"

Rita loves the sound of a fight brewing as eagerly as she loves pointing out all of my failings as a wife and mother, so it's predictable when she adds, "Now, Livvy, you need to feed this man better. After all his hard work he does to keep you home watching soaps and eating bon bons, it's the least you can do. Bradley, dear, do you want mommy to come over tomorrow and make you lunch for work? Oh, don't look so put out Livvy, I'm teasing."

The thing is, Rita you fucking bitch, you're not just teasing.

Okay, truth? I used the words 'fucking cunt.' But I have never used that word. Bradley does, though. Often. Now it's seeped into my vocabulary along with the F-Bombs.

Hey, Rita, thanks for teaching your son to use that same bullshit line every time he says something rude or derogatory or plain fucking offensive.

My tone is all tolerance and forbearing. "Of *course*, you are, Rita. Bradley, it'll be ready in five minutes."

"Ma, what the fuck. Liv feeds me, don't worry."

Wow, you're sticking up for me? To your mother?

"She feeds me burnt fucking cutlets and some nasty green shit."

They both laugh, and laugh, and laugh at that one. Like two braying donkeys. Did I really imagine he was going to stick up for me? Even though it's pointless, and neither

94

one is listening, I can't help announce, "Kale. It's kale, and it's good for you."

Believe it or not, I'm not actually mad that he didn't defend me. It's worse when he does, because it's always over the top and dramatic, then they don't speak to each other for a week, and somehow, I end up feeling bad. Like I'm the asshole. Thanks to my husband, his mother has always thought I was a prima donna.

We'd dated for about a month when I went to dinner for the first time over his parent's house. Thick fatty steaks as big as the plate itself with a gallon of iodized salt and a side of ketchup, canned corn, and white rice, no salad. Joe, his dad, plopped a rare slab of meat on my plate, and before I realized what was happening, Brad had reached over me, with his knife and fork in hand, and proceeded — to everyone's astonishment — to cut my steak into tiny child sized bites for me.

Rita, all six-feet of her, practically fell out of her chair as she hooted and guffawed, "Aww, wook at the wittle princess. Is the knife too big for your wittle hand? Big Bradley gotta cut it all up for you?"

Hardy-har-har, guffaws all around the table. Rita, Joe — first thing I'd heard from him that night — his older brother Karl and the traitor and instigator of the whole ridiculous scene, Bradley. To this day, I can't imagine what ever possessed him to do something so bizarre. Since then, she's had the impression that *I* think I'm a fragile doll who must be taken care of, when in fact it is her son who thinks it. He always has.

But again, I can take my share of the blame here. Again, I can say that, in the beginning, and aside for the steak incident, I liked it. Yup, like an idiot, I ate it up. Truth be told, people have always treated me like that, like I'm some kind of doll. Underestimated me. Maybe it's my height, or they mistake my natural reserve for shyness, I don't know. But I'm not above admitting that I'd sometimes used it (often, I'd used it often, okay?) to my advantage growing up. I let people do things for me and speak for me.

No one, save my drama teacher, Mr. McRand, saw past the exterior. He encouraged me to go to California after graduation and follow my dream of acting. At least, that was my plan before Bradley Handler. Mister, as we called him, seemed to be the only one who looked hard enough and deep enough to see something more in me. He always pushed me to be more, try harder, and be braver, stronger and tougher than I felt. It worked, for a while. I haven't felt so strong these last couple of years though.

Congratulations. Mission accomplished, Bradley. You wore me down, wore me out.

Mostly, but not completely. I remember how he used to get me to cry. Back in the early days. He knew my weak spots. And that's where he'd poke and jab and cut away at. But I'm a quick learner, too. Making me cry made him feel like the big man, Mr. Fucking Big Shot, like he held all the power, so I learned how to shut that side of myself down. Stopped showing weakness. I am like an emotional brick fucking wall, and him? Bradley is the big bad wolf that keeps huffing and puffing outside my door. But he will not blow down this house. He won't knock these walls down ever again. How's that for toughness, Mr. McRand?

There is one weakness. One small, blonde haired piece of Kryptonite coursing through my veins and keeping me under his thumb. Kadee. He and I both know I'll do nothing to jeopardize her stability, her security. He's made it clear. If I ever try to leave, he'll make life a living hell. Sealed with a promise. Then he laughed, and said "Aww, now don't get so mad, I'm teasin' you, Liv. It's not like you're planning on leaving me — *us*, now are you? Hmm, are you

Liv? C'mon, like, really? Where would you go, right? No college education. No money. No car. Ya got nothin' Liv. No, Princess Livvy is not going anywhere, anytime, are ya?"

He anticipated he'd get me to cry. He almost got me. Almost. But I waited. I watched from the wide living room window, rocking and bouncing Kadee to sleep as he rooster strutted and whistled down the front steps to his black Lexus. I waited and watched and squinted against the sudden glare of the sun off the driver's side-view mirror when he opened the car door.

I stood and rocked and waited until he backed out, waving at us in the window like Ward fucking Cleaver, waited till the brake lights flicked off and he turned off Marshall and onto Harvest Lane, heading towards the highway onramp, waited until I'd set Kadee in her crib, turning on the ocean sound effects machine and clicking the baby monitor on before closing her door. Then I waited until I was in the bathroom, with the water running and a damp towel over my face, before I allowed myself to cry.

He'd love to know how hard I cried that day. It was the last time I did. He'd like to know my chest hurt after, and I had to take three aspirin and keep the cold wet washcloth over my eyes to bring down the swelling in my tear ravaged eyes the whole time Kadee slept. He'd especially love to know that the last piece of defiance and hope of freedom I'd been holding onto finally got locked away and replaced by a resolve to stay.

You won that day, Bradley, but you weren't aware of it.

He still thinks he has to keep knocking me back down into place. But then, I guess he does, huh? Because yesterday? Well, yesterday I had a glimmer of hope. Yesterday was Jack Weller. Something I at first felt guilty about. But today? Today I am glad. Wickedly, viciously glad. I got something past Brad Handler, right under his narrow nose. That would sure wipe the smug expression off his face. Prick.

Jesus Christ. This is who I am now. A mean, hard-hearted shrew, thinking mean thoughts in my dirt streaked shorts, standing in the cold air of my — *your, everything is yours* — refrigerator not remembering why I opened it in the first place because I'm too busy daydreaming about Jack Weller. Brad kills the thought easily enough.

"Uh, hel-LLOO? Liv, you frickin' spacin' out in there? You get confused and think that's the TV? Duhhh, my name is O-di-via Hand-wer and I am a mo-ron."

Rita pipes in, "Duhh, how do refrigerators work? I'm blonde."

"Ahh, you two are fun-*ny*. I was looking for the ketchup."

For your potato salad. You fucking freaks.

Why, oh, why did Kadee have to fall asleep on the way home? It's too late to call my mother, too. How the hell am I going to get through the next two hours with Rita and him, her clone? Except for the height. He didn't get that from her. Instead, both he and his brother got their father's average stature. It would be funny that Rita towers over all of them if it weren't for the fact that she also uses psychological dominance on all three. From the counter, I hear my cell phone vibrating, as do they. For a split second, I have a shock wave of fear shoot through my chest, what if it's Jack Weller? As fast as it came, the worry is gone. Jack would neither have my number nor dare call it. Nonetheless, I've jumped towards it, and he noticed.

"Whoa, whoa, there, Liv. You expecting an important call? Your boyfriend, maybe? Damn, you don't jump that fast to answer my calls, that's for sure."

"Uh-oh, Olivia's in trouble."

Wow, Rita, could you have said that with any more glee?

I ignore her and roll my eyes at him, "Oh, my God Bradley, seriously?"

Brad says, "How about if I check it for you, hmm? No reason I can't check your phone, right Liv?"

"Knock yourself out, Bradley." I feign indifference and continue pulling items out of the fridge and setting them on the kitchen island. Rita sits at the kitchen table with her beady hawk eyes glinting as brightly as her red nail polish as she watches the two of us like a tennis match. But I watch Brad from the corner of my eye, waiting to read his expression as he reads the screen.

"Oh, for fuck's sake, it's your pain in the ass big mouth friend. What's her name. Big boobs."

Instead of handing me the phone, he drops it back down on the counter. I sigh and walk to the counter to pick it up. I'm dying to hear what she has to say about yesterday, but won't ask until tomorrow when we go for coffee while the kids are at preschool. Three days a week, eight-fifteen a.m. to eleven-forty-five a.m. Mommy time. Me time. Still, it's odd she's calling on a Sunday, when she knows he's home.

"Liv, what the fuck? Whatever the gossip of the day is, it can wait. You're on my time right now, so leave it."

Two years ago, hell maybe even just last year, I'd have said *'Fuck you, Bradley'* and answered the phone. Instead, I stop in mid stride, and go back to the kitchen island and gather the plates and forks without a word. I see the two of them — frick and frack — exchange looks. His, smug and proud. Hers, impressed.

Breathe, Livvy, breathe.

NINE *COFFEE WITH THE GIRLS*

8:25 A.M.

"Let me guess, you couldn't answer the phone because Mr. Happy Pants was home."

"Ding, ding, ding. Give the lady a prize. Yes, Bradley was home, and even better, Rita was over."

"Oh, Jesus. How'd that go? Holy shit," Jan shakes her head, "that *woman*. Remember at, what was it? Kadee's second birthday? You guys spiked the iced tea, and she didn't know and, oh my God, I'm dying all over again."

Jan doubles over and laughs. Thanks to my mother-in-law's accidental drunkenness, Rita's polka-dot granny panties remain forever burned into everyone's retinas. We both double over laughing, recalling the sight of that massive woman, heels-over-head, flipped onto the grass. Not only did she not realize the iced tea was spiked, she was oblivious of the flimsy resin chair's precarious state.

Brad was livid, both at her and at his father, even his brother. For once, he wasn't mad at me. I was blameless, as it was he who made the spiked tea, he who labeled it, and his mother who did not read the sign taped to the pitcher, written in his clunky script: **SPIKED**.

"Oh, Jan, I doubt anyone from that day has forgotten. Remember Bradley's face? I swear to God steam came out of his ears."

At the mention of my horrid husband, our laughter dies off. He has that effect, even when not around. It's quite a skill. Timing is right, though, and it's our turn to order our overpriced coffees from the Goth Barbie Barista named Cheyenne, who acts like every time is the first time she's seen us even though we are there every single Monday. We place our orders, stake a claim to a corner table, and pull three extra chairs over. A few patrons dart annoyed stares and Jan glares back at them.

Mary, Karla and another preschool mom are joining us, but we arrive first, as planned. Now that we have the chance, I feel hesitant and don't have a clue how to start. What does Jan know? What is she thinking? As always with Jan, there's no preamble and I don't have to wait long. She starts right in.

"So, what's up with you and the hot DCD?"

"DCD? What? Oh, Day Care Dad, I get it. Ha, good one, that is definitely a good one."

I'm stalling, and Jan knows it. She also knows we have about ten minutes to talk before the others arrive, so she dives in.

"Listen, kiddo. I'm sure you don't need me to tell you to be careful here, do you? I mean, can I be honest? Bradley is a fucking asshole. You don't have to say it, I know it. Remember, my cousin Linda graduated with him, so I heard his story from her. If we hadn't fallen out of touch after school, I'd have warned your ass before you got mixed up. Not that you'd have listened. You were a stubborn shit then, and you're still one now."

Jan pauses long enough to grab both our coffees when Cheyenne mispronounces both our names — Jon, Libby — and returns, picking up right where she left off.

"The second I saw you looking at that hot DCD Jack Weller, and him looking at you, I knew it was trouble. I *knew* it. That guy is trouble for you, mark my words."

"Oh no. You said 'mark my words.' Damn it, Jan, you've cursed me."

I'm trying, half-heartedly, to make light. But history has shown that every single time Jan has ever said the phrase 'mark my words' it's been prophetic. She is not having any of it. As she eyes the door for our companions, she gives me her not so surprising perspective on Jack Weller.

"Listen I'm not saying I wouldn't take a romp in the sheets with the guy, I mean he is totally hot as hell for a guy his age. But, I'm a widow, and I can do whatever I want. You — *you* cannot. I mean, never mind the moral part and the whole you-took-vows thing. Wait, I don't mean *never mind*. You know what I mean. I'm just saying two words. Jessica Miller. You remember what happened to *her*, don't you?"

I roll my eyes at Jan. Nothing *happened* to Brad's ex-girlfriend. Granted, the story is weird, but she left town, that's all. Abruptly. In the middle of the night. However, she is not buried in some trash heap on the outskirts of town, as Jan is implying. I've never heard Brad once

106

mention her name, and no one speaks of her around him, except that one time when we met up with Dan Bannett and his mail-order bride at Alejandro's. It was that last round of drinks that loosened Dan's lips even more than they usually were, and he slurred,

"So Bad — Brad, didja ever tell Livvy here about Jess? Huh? Didja? Livs, I bet he didn't. Oh, ho ho, Did I strike a nerve, old buddy? I'll tell ya, I'll tell ya, Liv. Sit here next to your Uncle Danny. Come on, come on, I won't bite. Will I Song Li?" Insert lecherous laugh here. "So, our boy Bradley here was hot and heavy with Jessica Miller throughout senior year. Her parents did not like you, bro. Am I right? Anyhow, everyone expects these two are going end up married, they're like, inseparable. Wherever Jess was, Bradley was right there. Bam. But — an' here's the kicker — the day after graduation, I mean the very next day, BOOM. The Millers are gone. G-O-N-E, gone. Packed up everything they owned and left town, never to be seen or heard from again. POOF. Old Bradley was *all* kinds of out of sorts, weren't you, bro? Bro? Hey, where'd he go?"

At some point during the story, Brad had walked out, gotten the car and when he walked back in, his face was like thunder. Until he turned to Dan Bannett and plastered a salesman's smile on his pasty face and bellowed, "Good times, bro, good times. Listen, we've gotta fly, the sitter called and the kid's fussin.' You know how it is with kids. Great seeing you, we'll have to do it again sometime."

Before Dan could even finish saying, "Give me your number, bro," we were out the door. He even held the car door for me, a first. Although, he almost slammed my leg in it in his hurry to get the hell out of there. The car ride home was morgue silent. I didn't even dare reach for the radio dial even though I was dying to hear anything but the sound of heavy breathing from the driver's side. This was the first I'd ever heard of Jessica Miller, but not the last.

"Yes, Jan I remember the Jessica Miller story. You don't have to worry. Nothing happened, nothing *will* happen. I doubt I'll even see Jack Weller again, anyhow. We're on opposite sides of town, so we will not be running into each other, anyhow. No worries."

"Um, yeah, about that? When Mary had said he's renting the house on Bartlett Street? Well, while you were outside on the phone with Mr. Misery, and we were ordering another round of drinks, Hot DCD Jack corrected her. He's renting the house on Bar*nett* Street, not Bart*lett*. Two streets over from you."

I open my mouth to speak, but nothing comes out. Jack Weller lives in my neighborhood, a mere two streets over. Fuck. There was no time to react, the other women had arrived. So, we do what we do. Drink coffee, talk about our kids, make plans, exchange recipes, and all things cliché. That's not a complaint, mind you. I love it. I feel like I am a part of something, instead of isolated and adrift. This is all thanks to Kadee. She is my tether to the rest of the world, one that Bradley can't stop or control. At least not completely.

In fairness, most of my days are free. Bradley leaves every day at the crack of dawn, and doesn't return until dusk, sometimes later. He travels the state, peddling drugs — ha, pharmaceuticals — to doctor's offices, wearing an expensive looking suit and shiny shoes. He wears his thin, dirt-blond hair slicked back because he thinks it makes him look like Bradley Cooper. At best he resembles Bradley Cooper's overweight cousin. Distant cousin. Who's an asshole.

The Bradster, as he's referred to himself as, enjoys schmoozing with doctors it makes him feel important. At every party, every get together, he tells everyone about 'my buddy, Dr. So-and-So' or how 'me and Dr. Blah-Blah were recently discussing this innovative medicine that will change the way we treat Diabetes.' Or heart disease. Whatever. I've stopped listening long ago. Another thing I wished he'd stop doing? He acts like *he's* a doctor, and not just a drug rep. It makes me anxious and embarrassed because he's always giving unsolicited medical advice and handing out free pill samples.

He has no idea what people should or shouldn't be taking, yet he hands them out like candy. I'm terrified that someone will get sick or die even from taking something he's given them. And then when the police investigate — or someone sues — we'll lose everything and be in the news, and God knows what else.

I've asked him to stop. Many times. I told him my fears and concerns and even made the foolish mistake to disparage the drug industry for its greed and contribution to an over medicated society.

Of course, he scoffed at my worries, made fun of my fears and was quick to point out I don't seem to mind the lifestyle this 'drug industry' has afforded us. I had no rebuttal. He's right. Not that I said that aloud. But he's right. I've fallen in love with this life as much as I've fallen *out* of love with him.

Wow. Love and Bradley. I haven't considered those words paired in ages. What did that feel like? You know what? I can't even recall. His persona, appearance, his smell, and vulgarity, meanness, and classlessness... his breath — all of it has erased any trace of any love I may have felt once upon a time.

More truth? I don't believe I ever loved him. He bowled me over and overpowered me with his larger-than-life personality. Swept up into his tidal wave. I floundered, unsure of what my next step in life was. College? Pursue acting? Writing? Hop a bus to California and chase a dream?

This scared, small-town girl had no clue. I couldn't stay at the day care forever, flirting with a technically still married man more than twice my age. Then, out of nowhere, Bradley Handler swooped in and took over my life. A chance crossing in a convenience store doorway. I was going in, he was coming out. He grabbed my arm as we side-stepped each other and announced to the entire store and everyone in the parking lot he had just met his future wife. Yelled it. Twice.

He asked where I'd like to go for our first date. He hadn't even told me his name yet. I didn't find Brad attractive, not at first. But he grew on me. Like a fungus, I now think... wryly. But then? Well, he was kind of funny, in a shocking way. He was also totally, completely, and undeniably different from anyone I'd ever met. I saw it as a sign. And it was. I just read it wrong.

There's been times when I've told myself he can't possibly love me, either. He doesn't even *know* me. He only believes what he wants to believe, what he wants to see. Tiny, easy to manage Livvy. Shut up and look pretty — but not too pretty — when we go out Livvy. Cook me dinner Livvy. Do the cleaning, take care of the kid Livvy.

Bradley wouldn't like an 'I can do it myself Livvy', or 'strong Livvy.' He wouldn't want that Livvy because it doesn't fit his ideal. And in his defense, I'm not sure how much of those 'Livvys' had developed yet. *Have* developed yet.

I suppose strong, independent, and self-sufficient Livvy was hiding below the surface, dormant. In wait for the perfect moment to burst from the earth and stretch toward the sunlight. Only, Bradley came along and eclipsed the sun. He *mimicked* the sun and tricked me into following his light only so he could cast me into his shade.

If we'd dated longer — more than the six months before our little 'surprise' happened — we'd have broken up. I would have seen the faults in my judgment and moved on. I'm confident of this. But then, we wouldn't have sweet Kadee. So here we are. Two people who don't belong together but are.

TEN *NEXT ORDER OF BUSINESS*

9:50 A.M.

Coffee finished, I leave the ladies at the coffee shop. Jan and I promise to catch up again a little later in the day. We both have errands to run before grabbing the kids from preschool at eleven-forty-five, but thankfully she doesn't ask where I'm going. It's not like I'm going to meet up with Jack, but somehow, I still feel like I'm about to commit a criminal act.

My plan — silly as it is — is to run across town to the Book Haven, the old family run bookstore from the past. My talk with Jack Weller had brought back the memory of my love for that coveted book that I never got. To hope they'd still have a copy for sale seemed too ridiculous, yet I had my fingers crossed. If not, I would have to search for it online and have it sent, but I don't want Brad to get the mail and ask questions. I don't *actually* think he'll remember the book, or its significance, but I'm not taking any chances.

Every birthday and holiday, my father sends me a check in lieu of a phone call, visit, or any other semblance of fatherly affection, so I have a secret stash of cash for those occasions when I don't feel like answering to my husband for every single purchase.

There are three places he'd never search through. My bookshelf, my tampon box, and the pot & pan cabinet. That is where I hide my treasures, almost in plain sight in the case of the bookshelf.

It is also where the new/old book will go, assuming I locate it, and he'll look right through it as if it's not even there. Books are not a Brad 'thing' as he likes to say. Married With Children DVDs and reruns of MASH are, however. Oh, wait, he does read, though, Playboy — for the articles, ahem — and Hustler, because he 'likes big tits, and I'm the leader of the itty-bitty titty committee.' His words, of course.

ELEVEN *CHARLI AND THE BOOK HAVEN*

10:12 A.M.

Traffic is light, and I arrive across town at the old bookstore in excellent time. There's parking available in front of the building — one long row of slanted lines marking the spaces for each business — but I opt to go around back.

The Book Haven shares the quaint three business building with a flower shop and boutique for people who like to spend stupid amounts of money on designer children's clothing that the kids will grow out of in two weeks. Kadee has three outfits from there, all bought by Rita. She made sure to tell us how much she spent on each one and expressed her hope that I would figure out how to wash them without ruining them. And suggesting I preserve them, for 'the next one.' And that I make sure I put an undershirt on Kadee first because she knows how I tend to 'let the poor thing freeze.' Oh, and that she probably would freeze less if I 'put some meat on her bones', instead of feeding her 'that rabbit food' I like to make. As usual, I smile politely and thank her.

Anyhow, I've never even been in there, and have no interest. The flower shop sign reads Charli's Flowers in faded gold script against brown weathered wood. Garlands of silk wildflowers frame the window and an arch made from birch branches curves over the door. It's charming and quaint. So much so, I promise myself a bouquet of wildflowers for the kitchen table. And seed packets to grow my own around the vegetable garden. But first, the bookstore.

The moment I step through the door, a wave of nostalgia washes over me. The smell of old books and fresh coffee mingles with lemon-scented polish on the warm wood floors. There's a working phonograph in the back corner playing a scratchy vinyl from the 1940s and a dress form with a colorful scarf, wide-brimmed hat and pearls. Beside it, a sign that says,

Come On Over and See Me Sometime

(But don't touch, please.)

-management.

Everything is the same as it ever was, from the heavily scarred, deep seated leather chairs that punctuated the rows of bookcases, to heavily made-up Rosalinde behind the counter, reading a book. From the looks of it, it was something to do with mysticism and crystal healing. Everything about the old bookstore was eclectic and welcoming, and I realize now how much I've missed it.

"Livvy? Olivia Perry is that you?"

The familiar sound of Rosie's rich throaty voice. She remembers me. Inexplicably, my eyes sting, and I blink hard.

"It's me, Rosie. How've you been?"

"Well, bless your heart, Livvy. I'm just fine. But, how are *you*? How long has it been? Three years? No, four. Tell me it's not more than that, mercy me. My word, is it possible you've gotten smaller? Lord knows I haven't."

Rosie laughs off her own comment, she has put on weight and isn't looking to deny it or have anyone else deny it. In a flash she's come around the counter and gives me a warm, back thumping hug. She takes both of my hands, turning the palms up for inspection. Rosie has always fancied herself a bit of a psychic who dabbles in clairvoyance and believed she'd had numerous past lives.

"Hmmm. Things not so good, are they? Hold on, hold on. Don't tell me. Just a moment now, the spirits are talking to me here, Livvy."

I wait patiently, intrigued despite myself. I mean, I'm not a cynic, but I'm also not completely sold. Still... if she can help. Ugh. Listening to the thoughts in my head right now — I reek of desperation. That's probably what she senses more than anything. But instead of a dramatic, 'I see blah blah blah in your future' spiel, Rosie surprises me with a funny tight smile that doesn't reach her eyes, and says, "Aww, well. Let's never mind that now. Hey. I have something for you."

I'm confused; how and why would Rosalinde Bookhaven — yes, that's really her name, she had her name legally changed from Weller to Bookhaven. At least I think she did it legally — have something for me? She had no way of knowing I'd be coming in today... or did she? Perhaps she really *is* psychic after all.

She disappears behind the counter, rummaging through the shelves below the register and muttering, "It's here somewhere," and other, unintelligible utterances in the same vein. Then, with a self-satisfied flourish, says, "Ah-ha. Here it is. This, my dear, is for you."

Rosie smiles kindly as she presses the book — *the* book — into my hands. It is the exact one from all those years ago, and I know this because of the crumple at the bottom right corner. Some careless person had dropped it long ago, but I hadn't cared back then, nor do I care right now. But I still don't understand how she knew I'd be coming in to buy this very book on this very day.

"Liv, honey, I've been holding that book for you for a long time now."

"But Rosie, how? Why? You weren't even here the day I came to buy... oh." Realization has dawned on me, but I still refuse to believe that what I'm thinking is true. I search Rosie's face for confirmation.

"Yes, Livvy. It was Jack. My cousin had quite a soft spot for you back when, but I'm sure you already know that."

I blush.

"Now, now. No need to get embarrassed. Jack was — still is a handsome man. Ladies have loved him from the time he was a boy. He's got that Weller charm. That's my dad's side of the family. But he never paid any mind to that kind of stuff, always humble. But you, *you* got under his skin, kiddo. Had him acting like a love struck boy, you did. Never seen him act like that before. Not even with what's her name."

His ex-wife. The first one.

"You mean Jack bought this book for me, thinking I'd return for it?"

"Looks like he was right, after all, now, wasn't he? Better late than never, and it's never too late is what I always say, Liv."

I'm dumbstruck, and suddenly conscious that I've been clutching the book to my chest, practically embracing the damn thing. I thank her and after some small talk I awkwardly purchase a few unneeded and random knickknacks at the counter.

Finally, we say our goodbyes, I promise to not be such a stranger anymore. Once back in my car, I can finally allow myself to look down at the leather-bound tome. There is a fine layer of dust on the cover that I brush away thoughtlessly with the side of my shirt sleeve before opening it to the first page. It is then that I see the rectangular scrap of paper wedged in the binding. On it, this,

Lo,

-H.H.

It means, 'To Lolita, from Humbert Humbert.' A private joke between a forty-one-year-old man and a seventeen-year-old girl that wasn't entirely a joke. I take the yellowed scrap of paper and hold it to my lips for a second before relocating it deep in the book's center, where it will be better hidden.

Instinctively, my eyes dart around to see if Brad is somewhere lurking about, watching me. But there's no one around but me and who I'm guessing to be Charli of Charli's Flowers unloading plants and buckets of loose flowers from the back of a white van. She's an older woman. I'd guess late fifties, early sixties with fiery red hair and a strong farm build. Still the buckets appear heavy and the work laborious and I see her struggling. I watch her carry one bucket in through the back door of the shop at a time. By the third trip, she was clearly exhausted. Yet no one came out from the shop to help her. Was she really by herself, doing all this work?

She stops for a moment, rests both hands on the back bumper of the van and bows her head. She's catching her breath. She looks so alone out there that I find myself setting the book down on the passenger seat and opening my car door. Before I've even thought about it, I've walked over to the van, grabbed a bucket and start walking it in through the back door and into what is obviously the workshop part of the store.

A wide deep sink and shelves of spray paint adorn one short wall, along with a corded telephone and order pads clipped to a clipboard. On the longest wall, the one that separates the showroom from the work room is a counter that runs the full length of the wall. Shelves of baskets, vases and other floral design paraphernalia cover every available shelf space, and from the lowest shelf is wire spool with every color ribbon known to man. Or at least known to me.

A rack of Swiss Army knives, plastic utility drawer unit with what appears to be wires, pins and floral tape, as well as a jar of scissors is dead center of the counter. It looks like a crafter's heaven, my kind of heaven.

I set the bucket down next to the other three and go back out to introduce myself. But the woman who I assume is Charli merely hands me another bucket and we continue on this way for about another ten minutes. We finish quickly, now that there are two instead of one doing the work. The woman eyes me, assessing me.

"Sturdy for a little thing, aren't you?"

I laugh and agree proudly.

"Name's Charli, like on the sign. You're Mo Perry's girl, right? Went to high school with her. 'Course that's when she went by Hauer, and Mo instead of Maureen."

She says it 'Mo-Reen.' I can't imagine anyone calling Maureen Perry by the nickname, it's so… so carefree sounding. Maureen is anything but carefree. She is a business-like woman and she always, always goes by Maureen.

"I am. My name is Olivia, but everyone calls me Livvy, or Liv. Those flowers — that work room — it looks so fun. You're so lucky."

Charli makes a sound somewhere between a snort and a chortle. "Oh, it's a blast alright. Especially when your arthritis acts up and you have twelve hundred roses to clean all by yourself."

"You do this all yourself? That's a lot of work."

Charli agrees, pretty much letting me know I've stated the obvious without saying a word. I'd dreamed of owning a flower shop once. I never told Brad that because he'd just laugh and say, 'well, add that to the list of Things Livvy Wants To Be When She Grows Up. Next, he'd shut it down with 'besides, you don't need to work, I give you whatever you need.' Or, 'Listen, you just sit back and look pretty and leave the thinking to me, will ya?'

How do I know? Because that's basically what he said when I mentioned I'd kind of like to go back to school. And when I said the local theater group placed an ad for set designers and actors. And the garden. And my... yeah, I had some ideas.

Charli surprises me with, "You lookin' for a job?"

"Oh, I — well. Are you looking to hire someone?"

"Hmph. I wasn't. But now I am. Got any skills? Besides lugging buckets bigger than you that is?"

I open my mouth to answer, but she goes on with, "Never mind, I can teach you. I could use some help making arrangements, cleaning flowers, customers... all of it I guess."

I want to. I really, really want to. What will he do if I decide right here and now to come work for this woman? Besides be mad as hell, of course. Oh, and then there's Kadee. My elation deflated. He would never agree to putting Kadee in full time day care, just so I could 'play with flowers' as he'd call it.

"I'd love to, Charli. You have no idea. But I—I have a little girl. She's three. I stay home with her and—"

"Bring her with. Plenty of stuff for her to do around here. Tomorrow, ten a.m. Sound good? We'll go over the details then. I only got part time available though. But holidays and funerals are my busy times, so I'll really need ya then."

Before I can stop myself, I agree to come back tomorrow and saying my thank you's and goodbyes for now. I'm practically skipping to my car, like a kid and I stop myself short when I remember, Bradley. He's going to try to sabotage this. But this is the second time in as many days where I've felt this almost unrecognizable surge of hope and excitement. He will not take this away from me.

TWELVE *PRESCHOOL PICKUP*

11:35 A.M.

Even after the whirlwind morning, I manage to get back to pick Kadee up in record time. Jan pulls in next to me and we walk in together. As we do, I tell her about my new job. "What? That's awesome, Liv. But, um, what about Big Bad Brad? How's he gonna take it?"

"I know. But any argument he has against it, I can counter. Kadee? She can come with. Gone from the house too much? It's only part time and won't interfere with dinner being on the table or the house clean, or God forbid

I'm not home when he gets there. Check, Check, and Check. I win."

Jan looks as dubious as I feel. Bradley has his ways, I'll give him that. But I'm not going down without a fight. At the sight of Kadee, paint in her hair, a smile on her face, and grass stains on her tights, I set all my worries aside.

The car ride home is spent listening to her recite everything she did at school and singing along to her favorite CD of the moment, and when we pull into the driveway, we mutually agree that ten minutes on the swing set is totally fair. Lunch and nap can wait. She's unaware of it, but we are celebrating mommy's victory. I have a job.

THIRTEEN *PREPARE FOR BATTLE*

5:25 P.M.

Dinner — Bradley's favorite — is prepared. Steak, potatoes, corn. The house is spotless, the laundry washed, dried, folded and put away. Kadee's playroom, immaculate. I've given her a bath, taken a shower and even put on a hint of makeup. All an obvious set up for a request that he'll see through instantly. I wash away a little of self revulsion I'm feeling with a gulp of wine, shoot a loathsome glance at the foyer mirror and tell my reflection, "You are a chicken shit coward. You know that?"

From behind me, Kadee giggles 'shicken shit' and runs off. Great. Just great. How is it that he walks around shouting things like 'mother fuckers' and 'son of a whore' and she repeats none of it, yet I let go one swear in three years — in front of her, that is — and, BOOM. There it is. Fuck.

I hear his car pull in the driveway, or rather his heavy metal music blaring from the speakers. I hate his music, but its volume means he's in his version of a good mood.

Okay, that's a good start. It means he is slightly less likely to say, 'what the fuck is all this.' Car door slams, keys jingle, back door opens and closes.

"Hey, there's Daddy's little girl. How's my baby girl today?"

Kadee runs to him and giggles, "Shicken Shit."

"What did you say, honey?"

She repeats it, louder.

"Livvy. You hear what your kid is saying in here?"

Well, shit. Not a good start. But when I go into the kitchen, I see that he's not mad. He is actually laughing, and telling her to say it again, but this time with his phone out and set to record video. What was I thinking?

Of *course*, he'd love for his child to swear. I want to admonish him, but I hold my tongue. I have to stay on his good side. So instead, I say,

"Hey, dinner's ready. You hungry?"

Ok, not sweet and loving, but civil, and in a nice tone of voice.

"Yeah, fucking starving. Why are we eating in here? Game's on."

"Well, I thought we could sit and have a nice family dinner tonight."

"Oh, crap. What do you want, Liv? This isn't about the God damn puppy again, is it?"

Well, that was quick. Stay calm, Livvy, stay calm. I get him a beer before I answer. I'm stalling, being chicken — *shicken* shit. He sits down at the table, before changing, without washing up first, but I ignore it and instead set a plate before him and get Kadee into her highchair.

"Napkin, Liv?"

Fucker, give me a minute, Jesus Christ. Don't you see I'm doing everything right now? You see the fucking napkins on the counter why can't you get your lazy ass up and get one?

No, I don't say this. I say, "Sure, coming right up."

As soon as I sit down, he says, "Ketchup?"

So, I go and get that, too. Physically biting my tongue. I've been rehearsing this moment, this conversation all damn day, and now I'm frozen. All three of us are eating quietly. At last, it's the sound of his chewing food that catapults me into abruptly speaking.

"I got offered a job today."

Bradley's fork hovered over the plate for a split second longer than the normal shovel, chomp, shovel routine, and he keeps his head down. Saying nothing. So, I try again,

"I said, I got offered a—"

"I heard you. So?"

Not, 'Doing what?' or 'That's great, Liv.' Just, 'So?' How do I still get surprised?

"So, I'd like to take it."

He inhales loudly, a slow whistling sound through his nose, and lets the air out just as slowly before setting the fork and knife down loudly on the plate. Both Kadee and I jump.

"Is that so? And what is it that you got hired to do, Liv? You gonna bag groceries over at the IGA? Walk Phil and Lisa's dog for them? What? What is it that you think you're qualified to do? Better yet, what are you going to do with the baby while you're out 'working'?"

Wow, Brad. You didn't even meter that out. Just BLAM. BLAM. BLAM. You know, when you pull out all the stops like that, it tells me you're nervous. Scared.

It dawns on me that this is what his reaction means. He's afraid. I need to keep calm here. Not let him provoke me. He wants tears, and he wants me to back off.

I'll be doing neither, Bradley. This time, I'm the one going in for the kill.

I feel this new calmness, and it might be the eye of the storm, but I am going to roll with it.

"Actually, Bradley, it's at the flower shop across town, Charli's Flowers. She needs part-time help, and I can even bring Kadee with me."

He's going to ask what I was doing across town, *there*. The Book Haven. I'm prepared. I see his eyes become little slits. Suspicious, mean little slits, but before he can ask, I tell a little white lie. Fine, a bold-faced lie.

"I ran into my mother in the grocery store and she asked me to go with her to the flower shop to pick out a centerpiece for the dining room table. She's having a dinner party — with some friends — I guess. She went to school with the owner and well…"

Stop there, Livvy. Talking too much, too much detail.

But Brad's picked up his fork again and has started stabbing the steak. Planning his next attack. He won't come right out and say that I can't take the job. He'll do about everything but that.

"And how do you think you're going to be able to keep up with everything around here? I don't want the house becoming a disaster because you have an urge to go play with stupid flowers. You already slacked off on the laundry this week. I had to go downstairs and match socks."

"Laundry is done and caught up, Bradley. I want to do this. I'll make it work. Besides, it'll be extra money and you won't have to give me any."

Risky argument, but I take my chances. He'll either be pissed that I'm implying we need the money, annoyed that I'm not dependent on him for cash — and therefore beholden — or he'll like the idea. I hold my breath and wait.

"So now I don't give you enough money? Is that what you're saying?"

Damn it. Time to backpedal. "No, Bradley, of course not. You're very generous." I almost vomit saying this, "I want to be more helpful to you. You work so hard, and I — I feel bad."

In my mind I'm making retching noises, outwardly I smile in a way that I hope looks demure and gentle. I'm not positive, but I swear he's beginning to sway.

"Hmph. I don't like you next door to that place. Does that fucker still work there?"

I cut my eyes to Kadee when he swears, but she is intent on her mashed potato masterpiece. It's everywhere, but I don't mind.

"What? Who? Oh, Bradley, please. I don't have the faintest idea who works in that place, nor do I care. Let's not be ridiculous, please. Anyhow, the flower shop is really cute, and she said she'll teach me how to make arrangements."

"Who else works there?"

"No one. It's just her, all by herself. That's why she needs the help. I saw her lugging these big buckets of flowers and I felt bad and helped her bring them in, and that's when she offered me a job."

"Thought you said you went there with your mother?"

Fuck.

"Yes, I did. You know my mother, impatient as always. When she — Charli — didn't come right out to serve us, she — my mother — sent me in the back to find her. And, then, well the rest is history."

Smile brightly. Stupidly. Bradley studies me from across the table; I can see the wheels turning behind those beady cold eyes, working up a new tactic. I'm getting anxious, I've only prepared for the ones he's already thrown out there. Think, Livvy, think. What's his next shot going to be? Turns out, it's an easy one. Bradley must be slipping.

"Well, I guess that means we won't be getting that puppy anytime soon, then. I mean, seriously, you'll be too busy to care for a kid, a dog, *and* have a job."

Okay, couple things here, Bradley. Low fucking blow, for one. You had no intentions of giving in on the dog request until this very moment. Another thing — I am not a fucking invalid. I can take care of more than one thing at a time. In fact, I do about ten times more things before ten A.M., than you do all day. So, fuck you.

"Well, Bradley, that's certainly up to you."

Oh, and guess what, Bradley? Two can play at this game.

"Kadee honey, Daddy says no doggie right now, okay?"

Kadee, like a broken record begins shouting "Kadee want doggie."

He tries to announce over her that we can't get a doggie because mommy wants to get a job, but she's hearing none of it. Since he can't handle her yelling, he shouts, "FINE. Fine, you win. Get the fucking dog, take the fucking job. But if this place starts going to hell, it's done, you quit. Got it? I'm going to watch the game."

I'm too stunned and giddy to answer, afraid that if I say one more word, he'll storm back in and say forget it, you're not doing it. So, instead, I do a quiet, seated victory dance that Kadee thinks is hysterical, so together we stomp our feet and wave our arms and celebrate.

From the living room he shouts, "You mind? I'm trying to watch the game out here."

We shush each other theatrically, whispering 'yay, yay, yay.' Kadee has no idea why we're doing this, but she loves it. So do I.

Three and a half hours later — well after Kadee had gone to bed — I accept the fact that he will be expecting more than a thank you for *allowing* me to accept the job at the flower shop. I say nothing when he tells me he'll take his shower *after* we 'do the deed.' I do nothing when he climbs on top of me like a lumbering bear and his full weight compresses my lungs, and I'm quite seriously struggling to inhale. I answer nothing when he grunts in my ear, 'touch yourself,' I comply. I know that as soon as I put my hand *down there*, and pretend to come he'll finish quickly, so I do.

My head taps rhythmically against the headboard. Neither of us adjusts the pillow so that it doesn't, and at last he finishes business in his predictable way, and all too slowly rolls off of me.

"Thata girl. Now go get me a washcloth, will ya?"

I throw my robe on, go to the master bathroom and grab a washcloth, tossing it onto his hairy, bloated belly as I hurry to the bathroom in the hallway. I turn the shower on, brush my teeth and then take a scalding hot shower, washing him off me and out of me, then switch the nozzle to fill the tub for a bath.

I feel sick and I feel violated. For as much as I am disgusted by him, I am so much more disgusted by me. That all too familiar panic rises up in me, that one that makes me scream inside, the one that says, *I can't live like this. I can't* and then counter argues in that calm dead voice, *I must. I have to. I chose the bed, and now I have to lie in it.* I start to hyperventilate, so I bite down on a towel and force myself to fill my mind with happy thoughts.

Kadee, comes to mind first. Next, the flower shop. The bookstore. The book. The Jack Weller. My eyes pop open. As I watch the steady drip from the tub faucet, I repeat those happy thoughts like they are my mantra until my breathing has steadied.

An hour and a half later, after peaking in on Kadee, I creep downstairs and out to the car, baby monitor in hand. Bradley is sound asleep, I can hear his snoring on the baby monitor. That's how loud he snores, that the baby monitor down the hall from our bedroom can pick up the sound.

I unlock the car doors, climb into the passenger seat, and lift the treasured book onto my lap. I sift through the pages until it falls on the one with the slip of thin paper wedged deep into the spine and place my finger over the '-H.H.' Jack Weller put his hand to this paper, perhaps pressing his own finger against 'Lo' all those years ago, before closing the book cover on the paper and handing it over to Rosie to hold for when I returned.

A brief thought to Bradley. Ironically, for as much as I despise him, I feel guilty. Yes, there's this side of me that is reveling in my secret fantasy world, but the guilt is present as well. Not that it matters, any of it really. I'm stuck. In this life. With him, for eternity. This here? This book, this slip of paper with four letters on it? It's just a dream. My little secret dream and it is going to have to be enough to get me through.

FOURTEEN *UNDER THE STREETLIGHT*

11:35 P.M.

The steady sound of Brad's snoring through the monitor is both annoying and reassuring. As much as I'd prefer the sound of silence, it tells me he's in a deep sleep and won't be bothering me anymore tonight. Once he's out, he's dead to the world.

After stashing the book under the passenger seat — I'll bring it in tomorrow and put on the bookshelf where it'll blend with the others — I climb out of the car and close the door quietly. The street is quiet, even Phil and Lisa's dog has called it quits for the night.

The sky is completely clear, and I gaze up into a million stars with renewed awe. The sight never ceases to amaze me, and even though I know it's so cliché thinking it, I wonder at how small it makes me feel. As I watch for shooting stars, I become aware of a distant tapping on the pavement.

It's a steady rhythm, rubber on concrete. I recognize it instantly as a jogger, something I used to be before Kadee was born. This had been my favorite time to run, too, and I smile at the figure as it draws near. Under each street lamp details immerge. Male. Blue and white running shoes. Flash of white headphone wires. Lean physique. His head comes up, beard. Oh, my God. My heart stops. Is it? Another lamp light illumination. Am I imagining this? No. It is Jack Weller jogging in the cool night — on my street — less than a driveway away.

He slows to a walk, stops at the end of the drive with his hands on his trim hips, breathing heavily. He slicks back the damp tendrils of hair from his forehead and watches me.

If he is surprised to see me standing there in my thigh-length robe, wet hair, and bare feet, he doesn't show it. I glance back at the house. Thankfully our bedroom window is on the opposite end and the light in the only window facing the driveway — the kitchen window — is on. If anyone were standing there, I'd see them. *Him*. I'd see Bradley if he were standing there. Silly of me to even panic over it. I can still hear the steady snore on the monitor clutched in my hand, which I turn down several notches.

"Hey."

A voice barely above a whisper, befitting the middle of the night. Still, it cuts through the air and through me with a jolt. Jack Weller says *'hey'* like it's the most natural, normal thing in the world to run into each other in the heart of night, in my driveway while my husband and daughter sleep upstairs. What do I do?

I say, just above a whisper as well, "Hey."

I walk to him. He has the sense to stay on the street and does not step foot onto my — *Bradley's* property. I act like it's a big deal, like there's some poignant show of respect happening. There's a smarter part of me that recognizes that there is no show of respect going on here. But I squash that smart girl insight like a pesky gnat. Even though the glow of the street lamp is a pale orange, it feels like a white-hot spotlight, and without acknowledging it we both side step away from its scalding rays and into the shadows. I glance around at the other houses, looking for nosy neighbors. All the while Jack Weller watches me but says nothing.

"Jack—" I begin, but I don't know what to say after that, and shake my head.

"I know, I'm sorry. I've tried to stay away, not come down this street. But tonight — I can't explain what happened, one minute I'm on Rutledge, the next—" He spreads his arms out, and looks around the street, my street. I get it. I really do. Since Jan had told me where he now lived, it had been taking every bit of will power to not take the long way home. I tell him this, not in so many words, but he understands.

"Livvy, honey, what are you doing outside at this hour... dressed like that?"

The way he says that word — *honey* — it's not condescending, it's affectionate. Gentle. Like being wrapped in a warm blanket when you're shivering. It makes me want to cross the literal line that separates the driveway from the road as much as the moral one that keeps me rooted to the spot.

"I was getting — " I stammered, "Jack, the book? I—I went to the bookstore today, and—"

"I heard. I stopped by earlier to see Rosie. She told me. You must think I'm some kind of—"

"*No.* No, Jack — I loved it. I love it, really. That's probably the sweetest thing anyone's ever done for me."

"Oh, little Livvy, someone should be doing sweet things for you every day."

What do I say to that? I'm speechless. I say nothing and look away. His eyes on me are intense. I can read him. I can read the desire, the pity, and the need. It overwhelms me like it did back when. What if I'd ignored my fear back then? What would've happened? For that matter, what would happen now, if I ignored every bit of sense and propriety and decency — not to mention loyalty — and let my feelings lead me?

I believe Jack Weller, with those eyes and that gentle sexy voice; he knows what I'm thinking. He knows I am on the verge of something than can't be undone. He says one word, and I swear to God, I feel it shoot though my chest and straight to my pelvis. All that word is, is "Livvy."

It's statement, a question. It's a calling, a whisper. A plea. I can't resist it, and as if there's an invisible cord pulling me forward, I take one step, then another towards Jack Weller. In my hand, the monitor sputters and crackles; I'm moving out of reception. I gaze down at it, confused for a moment, then realize where I am and what I was about to do.

Abruptly, I say, "Jack, I—I have to go."

I turn and run to the house, cutting through the wet grass. When I reach the door, I turn back to the street. Jack Weller is slowly jogging away, his head hung low. What the fuck am I doing?

FIFTEEN *FIRST DAY ON THE JOB*

2:15 P.M.

Kadee and I love the flower shop. Charli gave Kadee blocks of floral foam and a basket of broken flowers and let her make 'arrangements' for the display case. She did that practically all morning, until I fed her lunch, and then again after. By the end of our time there, she was starting to get fussy, but she hung in there like a trooper. Next time I'll remember to bring her little fold away cot for a nap.

I was so nervous that I had butterflies the whole day, but Charli says I'm a natural and a keeper. I'm embarrassed to admit it, but I preened and beamed as if I won a million dollars. She asked if I minded working 'under the table' and once she explained what that meant, I was thrilled. That would mean Brad would never know how much money I actually have. Another secret to add to the growing pile. We leave at two p.m. with a plan and a deal, I will come in three days a week, while Kadee is in preschool. She doesn't ask any personal questions, not even when Brad called and texted me a total of eight times. She raised her eyebrows and studied me with solemn eyes but held her tongue.

When Kadee and I get home — she's fallen asleep during the car ride — I am exhausted, but if anything's not exactly right in the house when Bradley gets there, it'll be enough cause for him to say 'I told you so' and that I can't handle the multiple responsibilities. I am not giving him that opportunity.

I bring Kadee up to her big girl bed, deciding that even though it was late for her to be napping, a short one would be fine. Plus, I felt like lying down for once, too. It's not yet three p.m., he won't be home until at least five-thirty. Later if traffic is bad. A nap would be heaven right now. Instead of leaving Kadee, I climb into her bed with her and fall almost instantly asleep.

SIXTEEN *DADDY'S HOME*

5:53 P.M.

The sound of a door slamming downstairs and key hitting the glass foyer table startle me from a sound sleep. I'm disoriented and dazed, until I look at my watch. Fuck. Kadee and I have been asleep in her bed for three hours. Brad is home, there's no dinner and I have no good excuse, not in his eyes at least.

"Seriously? One fucking day of work and you have to take a nap? Told you this was a bad idea."

He'd made it up the stairs before I could wake Kadee and climb out of bed, and with my disheveled hair and sleep puffy face, I can't even deny it.

"Relax, Bradley. Dinner will be ready in ten minutes. Why don't you take a shower while you wait?"

"Uh, because I don't want to take a shower right now, I want to eat my dinner right now."

He walks away, towards the bedroom breathing heavily and cursing, 'Jesus fucking Christ' in time with his heavy footsteps.

Secretly, though? He's glad. Glad that I fucked up because now he can hold this over my head. Once he's calmed down, he'll say, *'Well, Liv, I'd say the least you can do for screwing up is put out tonight. Or is that too much trouble for poor tired Livvy after her one day of work?'*

Sure enough, right after finishing a hastily put together dinner — one which I can admit is not my best work — and let go a rolling belch that makes Kadee laugh and me dry heave, he says almost exactly that.

But what I realize, and he does not, is that there is absolutely no way Kadee will be going to sleep at a reasonable time tonight after taking such a late and long nap this afternoon. And that means I am off the hook because he won't stay up past ten p.m. since he needs to be up and out the door by six-thirty in the morning. In my mind, I'm doing a big fat happy dance, but outwardly I nod at him, as if it's going to happen. Haha, sucker.

We've gotten through dinner and Brad's off to watch TV, Kadee and I stay in the kitchen and make her lunch for tomorrow at preschool, as well as mine for work. Work. A place I get to go to and be creative and free. Probably not how most people feel about their jobs, I suppose.

For the first time, I wonder if Bradley actually likes *his* job. Is he happy selling drugs? Does he like the people at the main office? Do they like him? I try to be objective. What would I think of him if I didn't know him as well as I do? It's no use. I can't get past the burping, the farting, the smells, his appearance, his meanness. It's possible that if I were a different kind of person, he would behave differently. But we are who we are, aren't we Bradley? I gaze down at Kadee's blonde head, watch her little hands as they painstakingly spread peanut butter onto the bread with the back of a spoon, singing softly to herself as she does. At least we did this together right, Bradley. We made this perfect little human.

My internal battle wages on as usual. I keep telling myself that I have to stick this out — this marriage out — for Kadee's sake. It's not fair to her to make her a statistic, another child from a broken home. *I* was from a broken home. My parents divorced when I was three, Kadee's age now. I don't really remember my parents together, but for vague hazy images of a tense and quiet house. But that could be planted thoughts from Maureen's mouth. All I know for certain, is that I barely have a relationship with my father, aside from the mandatory holiday and birthday calls or visits. I avoid having both Maureen and Edward at the same functions at the same time. The tension is thick, the barbs and jabs many, and my discomfort is through the roof. I don't want that for Kadee.

The other thing — the thing I hate to admit and that he knows full well — I'm afraid to leave. I'm afraid in every possible way. Do I really fear he'd physically hurt me if I took Kadee and left? No, not really. But he would be spiteful and nasty, and he would fight me for custody. Not because he wants to raise Kadee, but because it would kill me not to. It's like he's said many, many times. Without him, I'd have nothing. Everything is in his name. The house. The cars. There are *bills* in my name — how convenient — credit cards he opened for me, utilities with my name on them, but none of the assets. I wouldn't even have the money to retain a lawyer, and my pride won't allow me to ask either of my parents for help.

So, there it is. I am stuck here, in this pretty gilded cage, for as long as he is determined to keep me. I've thought of that, too. That he'll get tired of me, tired of begging for sex, tired of my obvious disgust. I find myself hoping he'll have an affair, and leave me alone. But he continues to be as obsessive as ever, growing more controlling instead of less.

SEVENTEEN *TAINTED FLOWERS*

5:47 A.M.

He's making as much noise as possible as he gets ready for work. It pisses him off that I am asleep while he is awake. It doesn't matter that it wasn't until eleven p.m. before Kadee finally went to sleep, or that she woke up three times during the night. He knows it, but doesn't care. *Well, Bradley, I'm not giving you the satisfaction.*

I make sure that my breathing looks regular and deep, I keep my arm over my face, so he won't see my eyelids flickering. And I listen and wait. Heavy footfalls on the wood floor fade out into the hallway, and he stops at Kadee's room. On the monitor I hear the rustle and crackle of him bending down to kiss her sleeping head goodbye. I forget this about Bradley. In my contempt and disgust that pervades my every fiber, I forget that he does deeply love our girl. I think of her always as mine, my little girl. But she is his too, and he loves her.

These are those fleeting moments that I see the better side of him. I remember that it exists, and I find myself making excuses for his behavior. It's what he learned, it was how he and his brother were raised, he doesn't know any different.

But it doesn't make it more tolerable, Brad.

It doesn't, no matter how I try to convince myself otherwise. It isn't until I'm sure he's gone that I get up and begin my morning. When I get down to the kitchen, after first stopping at Kadee's room and re-closing her door that he'd left open, I go straight to the coffee maker. I'm stopped by a piece of paper leaning against a vase of flowers.

Meant to give you this last night.

Congrats on job.

-Me

Well. That was unexpected. In the vase there's a plastic card holder poking out — one of those long-forked sticks

— with a rectangle flower shop envelope. I can feel that it's empty but flip it anyhow. In elegant forest green factory printed script is,

Charli's Flowers
~Weddings~Funerals~All Occasions~

Below that, the address, website, and phone number. He went to Charli's for the flowers. Of course, he did because why would he go to the flower shop at our side of town, which is conveniently on the way home from work? The reality of the gesture I'd thought was so nice now becomes crystal clear, he wanted to check up on me. Check my *story*.

I can easily picture it — him strutting into the shop like a rooster — demanding the best and most expensive bouquet in the store. He probably said, "Nothing but the best for my princess, that's what I say. But if it's more than five dollars, I don't want it." Then laughed at his own joke.

When Charli just stares at him — because that's exactly what she would do — he'd tell her he's messing with her, and oh-so-casually add 'oh, by the way, my wife says she works for you now.' Charli would of course confirm it, because it's true. He'd have automatically expected a discount, and when she gave none, he'd decide right then and there that she is a crotchety old bitch with a stick up her ass.

Is that how it went, Bradley?

Is that why he didn't mention it last night? Because he got served as they say? I'm half tempted to toss the flowers in the garbage. They're tainted now, just like that. But then I notice that all my favorite flowers are in it. Lisianthus and Delphinium, stock, asters, lilies, tulips and waxflower, asparagus fern and lemon leaves. Charli has made this especially for me, because she learned in one day of knowing me, what flowers I like. There is not a single rose, a carnation or daisy to be seen. Bradley Handler had no part in picking out this arrangement. I'm positive of this because those are exactly the flowers he'd have insisted on.

That's another conversation I can easily imagine. Him asking for those common flowers, her saying '*I know what she'll like.*' That must've made him livid — a stranger telling him they knew his wife's likes better than he did. He'd have no rebuttal, which would enrage him even more. I bet his nostrils flared, and his thin lips disappeared completely as he put on that tight fake smile and said, 'Have at it, sweetheart.' Bradley is not fond of 'opinionated' women. They shut him right up, fast. Only afterwards, when we're home alone, do I hear about all the things he would've said, should've said, but held back because — oh, I love this — because he's a gentleman.

I wait a half an hour, then text him thanks. If I text right away, he'll rightly accuse me of feigning sleep, and if I wait longer than the thirty minutes, he'll — rightly again — accuse me of being ungrateful. I've got this down to a science. After I hit send, I get a text from Charli.

Weather's gonna be crap today.

Come in tomorrow, instead?

After I respond with a 'sure, no problem,' I pour my coffee and shake off the hostile thoughts. It's going to be a perfect stay-at-home day with Kadee. Heavy rain in the forecast, just right for a pajama day and movies, books and games with Kadee-bear.

EIGHTEEN *THE PASTOR'S WIFE*

10:00 A.M.

I wasn't planning on showing up. Really, I wasn't. Okay, okay, bullshit. I call bullshit on myself. I didn't need Barb to persuade me to come back for planting the garden we'd dug. I didn't need to hear the desperation in her plea, I'd already decided. Actually, Bradley decided for me.

Turns out, ironically, he's playing golf with Pastor Ted and his brother the doctor in this weekend's tournament. Apparently, Barb had expected the pastor to be home this weekend, helping her with the community garden, and was none too happy when he begged off in favor of golf.

When it looked as if Barb was going to win the battle, Brad determined it was on me to occupy Barb and get her off the pastor's back, or rather, as he put it, *'let the guy have his balls back.'* I weakly argued that I couldn't bring Kadee, but he had already called his mother to babysit. I said I had tons to do around the house, he said it can wait. Funny how easy going he could be about those things when it worked to his advantage.

So, there we have it, and here I am, staring at the back of Jack Weller's sun-tanned neck as he places a small fledgling romaine lettuce plant into the hole I'd prepared. It's the three of us, Barb, Jack Weller, and I, under the warm sun in the middle of a big patch of subdivided dirt. Jan isn't coming, her son is sick. Mary has a dance recital for the twins, and Karla won't be here until noon. I think two things. *'My God, even the back of Jack Weller's neck is sexy'*, and *'What if Pastor Ted tells Brad who else is helping with the community garden?'*

I need to figure out a way to ask Barb this without raising suspicion, but for the life of me I don't know how. In the meantime, Jack Weller and I — under the unwitting direction of Barb Stellar — are working side by side with a sexual tension that might make these fragile plants explode from spontaneous combustion. We say little — at least nothing of significance — but there's a subtle flirtation. Elbow bumps and side glances, smirks and grins, and a cohesive easy pattern to our work. I dig the hole, he drops in the plant, and I pat the dirt around the mound. Repeat. We do rows and rows of this. Lettuce, Swiss chard, kale, and more lettuce. Next week will be peppers and eggplant and whatever else Barb wants to plant. This is less a community garden and more a 'Barb needed to have a project' than anything else.

Before I realize it, three hours have gone by, and we all mutually decide enough has been done for one day. Karla, who was last to arrive, is first to leave. Then there's this awkward *thing* between me, Barb and Jack Weller. We both want Barb to leave, but she is puttering around and stalling. When it's obvious that Barb is making no move to leave, Jack shoots me a quick apologetic shrug and announces that he's going to hit the road, he'll see us next Saturday. I'm both disappointed and relieved. This will give me a chance to feel out Barb. Before I can speak, though, Barb surprises me.

"Livvy, honey... can I speak frankly with you?"

"Of course, Barb. What is it? If it's about the plants, I swear, Charli insisted, no charge. She won't accept a dime."

"Oh — oh dear. Ah, no. I mean, yes, that's wonderful of her, we'll be sure to thank her tomorrow morning in Pastor Ted's sermon."

I try not to giggle at the inappropriate image that suddenly pops in my head of Barb and Pastor Ted making love. '*Oh, Pastor Ted, yes, yes, Pastor Ted...*' What the hell is wrong with me? Focus, focus. Poor Barb is struggling for words.

"Barb, you look like you're having a stroke, what is it?"

"Oh, Livvy, I'm just going to come right out and ask. Are you and Jack Weller... well, I mean, are you two...?"

Well, if that's Barb's way of coming right out and asking, I can only imagine what her beating around the bush sounds like. Nonetheless, I understand what she is asking, and I am mortified. I'm sure I turned ten shades of red as I stammered a response.

"Barb. Oh, my God. No. No, I — that is we..." I sigh. "Well, Barb if you must know, Jack Weller and I have some history, and well... wait. Why are you asking me that?"

"Oh, my. Livvy sweetheart... would you like to go for a drink? At my place that is. The men won't be home for hours, and you mentioned Bradley's mother has taken Kadee to the zoo..."

Well, she's got me there. Kind of impossible to refuse. Truthfully? She looks sympathetic, and not judgmental, like I'd have expected a pastor's wife to react to possible adultery. I want — I *need* to unburden to someone other than myself. I'm beginning to understand what Sybil felt like with all these voices in my head.

NINETEEN *CONFESSIONS*

2:30 P.M.

If I'd ever taken the time to imagine what Barb's house would look like, this would not have been it. Of course, in my imagination I'd picture an English cottage like in Pride and Prejudice with a neat picket fence with tea roses draped over the wood slats and ivy climbing the stone walls. Instead, a tidy colonial with a landscaped row of ornamental trees in front of the house, two-car garage and a flagpole stood before me. We walk in through the side entrance and get greeted by a very excited toy poodle named Lazarus.

"That's a big name for a little dog, Barb."

"Yes, yes. It means, God is my help." She takes my arm and gives it a squeeze as she says this, and I'm not sure how that makes me feel.

Embarrassed. Uncomfortable. Yes, those things, but also? I don't know... redeemed? Eh, no. That's not the word I want, too extreme. Damn my lack of religious upbringing. Whatever the case, I get what Barb is trying to say, and it's more than just telling me what her dog's name means.

She pours us each a generous glass of Pinot Grigio and nods me in the direction of the breakfast nook. It's old-fashioned looking and charming, as is the rest of the house — as much of it as I can see, at least — and completely opposite of our cold contemporary vaulted ceilings and granite counters. His style, not mine.

I dream of exposed beams and weathered wood, antique store treasures, deep soft leather couches and warm colors. Instead we have a living, dining, kitchen, and bedroom sets straight off the showroom floor. Brad's den — excuse me — his 'man-cave' is the only room that has anything close to antique in it, the old traditional style recliner from his mother's house, from where he sits with beer in hand and watches the races, the games, the reruns, and whatever the hell else he watches. We, Kadee and I, are not allowed in the man-cave, which suits both of us fine. He has no idea, but I have on several occasions gone in and opened his fire safe. The one he thinks I don't have the combination to. Three tries and *click*, I'm in. Either he thinks *I'm* that stupid, or he's just that stupid. Anyhow, I've been in it. Stack of cash, deed to house, titles to the cars, life insurance policies, birth certificates for all three of us, a bank account that he believes is secret, oh and that feathery-edged photo wedged far in the back.

You know the one, Bradley. Your ex-girlfriend in a wet white t-shirt and looking into the camera in what can only be described as embarrassment.

She's caught frozen in time raising her hand to cover her chest, but he — I'm assuming it was him — took the picture before she could. You know what makes that photograph obscene? Not that her small breasts are visible, but the fact that she is being exposed without her consent. I've never needed to ask about her, or her leaving town, because everything I needed to know was in that picture.

Barb puts the bottle back in the fridge and starts toward the table, turns back, reclaims the bottle and brings it to the table with her, setting it beside our glasses. I smile and raise mine to hers with a forced smile.

Barb begins, fortified by her first sip, it would seem. "I don't mean to pry, Livvy. Really, I don't. It's just — well, even last week — there was clearly something between you and Jack Weller, and then today... well, today I thought to myself, 'Barb Stellar, if you don't say something to this girl right now, you'll never forgive yourself.'

When I get nervous or uncomfortable, I get sarcastic and snarky. This moment is no different. "Well it's a good thing Jesus forgives everything, right?."

Barb half frowns, half smiles. Guess she didn't quite love that one. What do I say? Am I supposed to confess my sins- real and the ones in my head- or what? Should I tell Barb that I fantasized about Jack Weller in my bathtub, or that he came to see me in the middle of the night, in front of my house where my husband and daughter slept obliviously in their beds? Do I tell Barb Stellar, the pastor's wife, that I hate my husband with a violence that makes me question my sanity? I really do. But I can't say that to Barb. However, I do have to say something. So, I tell her some.

"Well, Barb, you're not totally wrong. There is something going on between Jack Weller and me. I mean, nothing has happened between us, but there are... feelings."

Barb takes a big gulp of wine as do I. Then I fill her in on the history between Jack and me. Then, after I drain my wine and she refills it, I describe what life is like with Bradley Handler. All of it. While Bradley and Pastor Ted play gold and drink beer and back slap one another like new old pals, I tell his wife every degrading, humiliated, embarrassing moment. How he repulses me, bullies me, and how I let him do it.

At the end of what has become my confessional, I say to her, "It's not him that I'm so mad at, it's me. I hate my cowardliness and my complacency. I hate my fear and willingness to do what's easiest instead of what's brave or right."

After all of that, my almost nonstop flood of words, Barb — looking not at all shocked, much to her credit — asks, "And how old were you when you met Bradley?"

When I tell her eighteen, and fresh out of high school, she sighs and looks out the kitchen window for a moment. I get the feeling she is debating what to say next. What she finally does say stuns me.

"I was married once before. Before Pastor Ted. I was young, like you. Eighteen, unsure of what I wanted to do next, very sheltered. My father was a pastor, too, like Ted. Ironic, yes? Well, I was headstrong, wanted to get out from under my father's thumb, be free and wild, for once in my life. So, I did. Started sneaking out, partying, having a good old time. One night I met Greg. He was older. Twenty-six to my very green eighteen. My goodness, I was so enamored. He told me everything I wanted to hear, he was the complete opposite of my father. Therefore, he was perfect. So I thought at the time. I brought him home to meet my parents. As you could guess, my father would have none of it. Forbid me to see Greg ever again. We eloped that night."

My jaw has dropped. I see Barb as if for the first time. She isn't some plain, staid pastor's wife, she's a woman with a history, a past. You never know what another's experiences are, do you?

"Oh, my God, Barb. What happened?"

"Well, as you can probably guess, Greg wasn't all he was cracked up to be. In fact, he was quite the bastard, if I must say. He called himself an 'out of work actor' when we met, turned out the only acting he'd ever done was with me. He was unemployed, lazy, and he was mean. But I didn't see all that when I'd met him, I just saw 'different' and that was enough for me. I won't bore you with all the details, but it took two long hard years and some help from my father to get Greg out of my life, and another three before I was willing to try dating again. Pastor Ted and I dated for three years before I'd accept his proposal. He was a patient, kind man. Still is. I took the long way around to find happiness, Livvy, that's for sure. Looks to me like you're doing the same. So, what I want to tell you, right here, right now is, you stop beating yourself up. Stop beating Bradley up, too." She puts her hand up to stop me though I've said nothing. "Don't get me wrong, from the sounds of him, even I'd like to kick his... well, you get what I mean. What I'm saying is, he is who he is. That won't likely change Livvy. You have to decide. Is this the life you want for you and your little girl? Because if it is, then you must learn to live it, tolerate and accept it. But if it isn't, and you want out? Well, you're going to have to live that as well, and it won't be easy. But, Livvy dear, you have to do this with integrity, either way. Not for anyone else but yourself. If you let this thing with Jack Weller get in the way of the things you need to do, then it can only end badly. I *know* this, Livvy. It's okay if Jack Weller is the thing that gets you to the next step, but — and forgive me for overstepping — he is not the one for you, dear.

Well, she had me all the way up to the last part. What if Jack *is* the one, and this is my chance? How does she know? She doesn't. Sure, neither do I, not really, but what if? Barb Stellar has given me a lot to ponder, that's true. But she can't predict the outcome of my situation just because hers was sort of similar. Despite my defensive feelings, I try not to show it and thank Barb for her advice and for sharing her story. Apparently, I'm no more an actor than Greg was.

"Livvy, I suppose you don't want to hear any of this right now. You probably think I can't possibly understand what you're going through. I want you to know, you can talk to me. Your secrets are safe here, consider it like a confessional."

"You guys do confession in your church? I didn't realize that."

Barb laughs and shakes her head at me like I've said something absurd.

"Oh, Livvy. No, dear we do not '*do confession*' at First Congregational. You've really never been inside, have you?"

Defensively, I tell her I have too been in the church. For a wedding. And a funeral. Okay, so I suppose I don't actually know anything about what they do.

"Honey, no pressure, but why don't you come by for tomorrow's sermon? We're non-denominational, all are welcome. It's really such a wonderful community, our church family. Even if you're not into the religion part of it, it'll do you good to be a part of something, and not so isolated all the time, hmm?"

"We'll see, Barb. Maybe. Hey, listen. Thank you. Really, I appreciate you listening to me whine and complain. I have to admit, I feel a bit better now. But, I have to ask you something…"

"Pastor Ted does not know about Jack Weller helping in the community garden. That's what you're concerned about. Am I right?"

I can't do justice to describe the relief I felt in that moment, but I think Barb understands it. We say our goodbyes, and though I feel a tinge of regret and embarrassment for sharing such personal information with someone who before now, was merely an acquaintance through Mary, I feel lighter than I have in ages.

TWENTY *BARNETT, NOT BARTLETT*

4:00 P.M.

Our neighborhood, a small community consisting of a total of sixty-four homes built by one builder over the course of four years, is made up of a series of interconnecting streets, lanes, roads and a cul-de-sac. Our street, Marshall Road, can be accessed three different ways, and much like Barb's analogy earlier, I always take the long way home. Barnett Street in on that longer route. I always liked passing the man-made pond on the left and catching sight of the ducks. Since finding out that Jack Weller lived on that street, I've been avoiding it. Until today. I'm not sure what makes me do it, but I'll blame Barb because it's easier than blaming my own lack of will power.

Which one is his? I shoot glances at each driveway as I roll past slowly. Suddenly, I realize that the man in faded jeans and a white shirt setting a sprinkler in the center of the yard is none other than Jack Weller. Well, I guess I know which place is his now, don't I? I'm mortified, and worse, caught. Jack stands up before I pass by, looks directly at me, and waves like this is the most natural thing in the world. I wave back, no denying that I see him, and he motions me to stop. Fuck. Yeah, I stop.

"Fancy seeing you here, Miss. Perry. Oh, wait, Handler, I mean. Mrs. Handler."

"Hello, Mr. Weller. Twice in one day, fancy that."

Oh, aren't we so cute and funny, flirting here in broad daylight? Can this get more wrong? Oh, wait, yes, of course it can. Here comes a young girl who is unmistakably Macy. Five years older, five years taller, but Macy without a doubt.

To him she says, in that peevish, put-out way pre-teen girls talk to their parents, "Uh, Dad, I thought you said you were going to bring me to Sarah's like an hour ago." Then to me, in that fake-polite way they talk to strangers they'd rather not be bothered with, "Hi, I'm Macy. Nice to meet

— hey, you look familiar." Bored, polite disinterest turns to curiosity.

"Hello, Macy. I'd recognize those freckles anywhere, how are you?"

"Miss. Livvy? Oh my gosh. Hi Miss. Livvy. You were like my favorite day care teacher ever. I'm good... except Dad here keeps promising to take me to my friend's house and keeps blowing me off."

"Macy. Language, please. I told you, I'm waiting for a conference call, can't leave until after that." He shrugs and shakes his head at me, 'kids these days' says that shrug.

"Well, then, how about Miss. Livvy can bring me? It's only one block over. I could totally walk but he won't let me."

"Oh, Macy, now that's rude. You can't ask Miss. Per-Mrs. Handler to drive you some—"

"Jack, it's fine, really. Hop in Macy. I'll bring you."

Of course, it's not fine, it's insane. Yet somehow, I am bringing Jack Weller's daughter to her friend's house just like that. Fortunately, there's no opportunity for questions from the girl, as she is busily chatting about everything she's been up to since I saw her last. Nearly five years ago. I can't help but wonder if this is a preview of what Kadee will be like in a few years. Damn, they talk fast at this age. When she bounces out of the car, she shouts an offer to babysit any time I need it, and this causes an almost instant pounding headache. I'm sure it has nothing to do with that half bottle of wine from earlier, though.

TWENTY-ONE *OH, RITA*

5:01 P.M.

I have barely enough time to shower and change before Rita comes through the kitchen door with a sleeping Kadee slung over her ample shoulder, huffing and puffing.

I exclaim, "Rita. I would've come out to the car to get her." *Then I could've gotten rid of you faster.* "Here, I'll take her."

Although Rita sounds as if she might have a heart attack on the kitchen floor, she wheezes, "Oh, no, no, no, Bradley's princess can sit back and relax. I can bring Kadee up to bed."

Ahh, Rita. You fucking bitter, vicious bitch, you.

"Actually, Rita, I'm going to wake her. It's too close to bedtime for her to be taking a nap, and she'll need to have dinner soon. But thanks." I practically spit out those last two words.

Yes, thank you Rita for undermining me, insulting me and feeding my kid garbage food all day, and then letting her pass out in the car knowing that she'll be up all night. Your son can thank you for his guaranteed no sex tonight.

Ha, now I am actually grateful to Rita. Free again. Predictably, she looks put out and pouty as I pull Kadee from her claws. She is hoping for an invitation to dinner, I know this as surely as my own name. Well, not happening. Not doing it. Nope.

"You're welcome to stay for dinner, if you want."

What the fuck. What the *fuck* is wrong with me? Why am I such a pushover? A wimp? It's no surprise when Rita pretends to contemplate the idea, as if it never even crossed her mind, then agrees, making it sound like she's doing me a favor.

"Oh, well. I suppose I could stay for a while and help you out with Kadee. I can give you some handy kitchen tips, too. You know, like how to make things the way Bradley likes them."

Count to ten. Don't respond. Concentrate on waking Kadee. Dumb fuck. It's my own fault. Thank God, Kadee's waking up cheerfully and I don't have to keep making awkward and irritating conversation with darling Rita. We will communicate through Kadee, in that weird way adults do when they don't actually want to talk to each other.

"Kadee, honey, did you tell Grandma that you drew a picture of an elephant in school?"

"Oh, did you Kadee?. Wonderful. Did you tell Mommy you got to see an elephant at the zoo today?"

"You did.. So cool, baby. Show Grandma how you do your elephant song, okay?"

This buys me enough time to pour a glass of wine, waggle the bottle in her direction, a wordless offer to which she nods emphatically. We both need fortification to get through this quality time together.

By the time Bradley arrives home, bloodshot eyes and disheveled, dinner is ready, Kadee's wide awake and singing every song she knows, and Rita and I are a bit sauced. She's extremely talkative when she drinks, so there's little pressure on me to work at conversation. A few well-placed questions, and she's off on a tangent. Brad looks pissed.

My first thought is, '*he knows.*' Take your pick from my list of offenses, there are quite a few piling up. My buzz dies instantly, and I can feel my blood pulsing in my brain. My fear is unfounded. Rightful guilt, but unfounded in this moment.

He drops his things down where he stands, not bothering to move the dirt and grass caked golf shoes to the mud room or pick the visor up from the floor, or the candy wrapper that drifted under the side table, for that matter. Nope, Bradley just walks in and announces, "I gotta take a shit. Hold dinner, while I empty the tank."

Oh. It was his '*I gotta take a shit*' face. I'm too relieved to be disgusted. Okay, well — of course I'm disgusted — I'm simply too relieved to say anything about it. Once he's returned, we sit down for a typical dinner. He and Mommy Dearest dominate the conversation. Kadee and I mostly observe. I clean up, with the 'help' of Kadee, Rita leaves (with a back handed Rita-style thank you) and Brad stomps off to the den to watch television. Just another day in paradise. Tomorrow is Sunday, and like most of our Sunday's together, it'll be a long one.

TWENTY-TWO *ANOTHER MONDAY FUN-DAY*

8:49 A.M.

All the kids are in preschool, the moms in the coffee shop. No chance to really catch up with Jan in private, but she's made it clear that she not waiting one day longer for an update. Fortunately, Bradley is working late tonight, so Jan and I agree a get together is in order this evening. Christian and Kadee will be happy to have a play date while we catch up, but for now I have enough time for a coffee and gossip before I have to go across town to work.

Work. I still can't believe I get to go to a flower shop, play with flowers and make arrangements, and get paid to do it. Amazing.

Brad's hoping I'll get bored with my new little hobby and eventually quit. Probably because he said, "Hey, Liv, when you get tired of dicking around at that dyke bitch's place, maybe next you can do some work around here for once."

That's his go to insult when he comes across a woman that doesn't succumb to his 'charms' or who dishes back what he doles out under the guise of good humor. He well aware neither Charli nor Jan are lesbians. They are, however and coincidentally, both widows.

He also knows perfectly well that I have not let the house go to shit — his words — and he's only being an asshole because I forgot to pick up his shirts from the dry cleaners and he had to get them himself. My punishment for said offense was a full day of snide, sarcastic comments.

"Hey, Liv, I was going to go get tickets to that show you wanted to see, *but I forgot.*" Then, "Well, Liv, I bet if George Fucking Clooney asked you to get his dry cleaning, you wouldn't forget that, would ya?"

Can't imagine why I couldn't wait for Monday to roll around. Oh, great, sarcasm. So like Bradley. I've pulled into the back lot of Charli's Flowers/Book Haven/ Peek-a-Boo's Boutique and I don't even recall the drive. Ridiculous. Now that I'm here, my hands unclench from the steering wheel and my shoulders roll down from my ears.

I haven't seen Charli yet, not since Bradley's unexpected visit to the shop, and I'm a bit anxious to hear what she thought of him. Not that she'll come right out with it. In fact, I'm not so sure she'd even mention him coming by if I don't bring it up first. She's not one of those nosy busy-body types, asking questions and giving side eye. In fact, she hardly asks any questions at all, aside from all things flower related. She's not very expressive or talkative, which suits me fine. It's peaceful here.

I wave to Rosie as I walk in; she's unlocking the back door of the bookstore.

"Well, hey there, Livvy. How's it going over there with Chatty Charli?"

She's being playfully sarcastic, of course. She and Charlie have shared the same building for more than twenty years and have an easy if not unusual friendship.

It was hard to find two people more opposite than these two. Scratch that, Bradley and I come in at a close second. Hell, maybe even a tie. Except the two women get along and respect each other's differences.

After Rosie and I chat for a moment, I go inside and put my apron on. Charli's on the phone, taking an order and gives me a wave and points to the order board. Every floral arrangement order gets written out on a slip of paper and pinned to the board, and we fill the orders and put them in the back of the green delivery van that Charli's brother, Zeek, drives around town. He speaks even less than Charli, and barely even tips his hat when he comes and goes.

I keep my cell phone on the counter where I can see it, and answer Brad's texts as discreetly as possible, but Charli notices. After a couple hours, in which he has texted about eight times

Only a little higher than your usual, Brad. I'm sure it's because you know I'm at work.

I catch Charli eying me, so I apologize.

"Sorry about the texts. It's my husband, he's…" I trail off because the only way to finish that sentence truthfully is, *'a jealous, overbearing, controlling asshole that hopes he'll get me fired.'*

185

Charli looks at me for a beat or two longer then simply says, "Mhmm."

As if nothing was said, she begins explaining the importance of a good, sharp, diagonal cut on a stem. It has to be so, otherwise the stems will get pinched and render them unable to drink water, and therefore die. I feel like there's some metaphor in all that, but then again, we are actually literally cutting flowers with sharp knives and jabbing them into wet floral foam, so yeah, it's probably a very literal lesson in floral design that I'm getting.

To my surprise, Charli is an avid soap opera watcher, and every morning she puts on the episode from the day before. Since I don't watch day time television, the show is foreign to me. However, it's pretty easy to follow the story lines, and one of them revolves around a busty, collagen filled woman named Marguerite.

Marguerite annoys the fuck out of me, which is pretty rotten, because her character is an abused spouse. The husband Blake — or Blaine, something like that — likes to smack her around and she's afraid to leave him, even though she is the wealthy one and he's her playboy penniless creep. It pisses me off that she takes the beat downs, and that she doesn't get rid of him, and I say as much to Charli. Or really, to the television.

"Oh, seriously, Marguerite? Stop letting that asshat beat you up. You can be free of him. If I had money like that, I'd..." I stop myself, embarrassed. Then to Charli, "I'm just saying, in the real world, if someone had the money to get the hell away from a creep like that, they would."

After a pause, one long enough that I think Charli isn't going to respond, she finally says, "Well, I'd guess she's as emotionally abused as much as physically. If someone beats you down emotionally, you probably get to thinkin' it's all you deserve. That's what bullies do. They knock down your self-confidence, your worth. Make you think you couldn't make it without them. Damn, they even make you believe you don't have any rights to anything, that if you leave them, you'll be a beggar on the street. I dunno, though. Just a thought."

It was the longest sentence I've heard her speak. And she wasn't done.

"Oh, by the way — met your husband last week. Interesting fellow, that one. Excuse me, gotta get the customer out front."

Conveniently, the bells attached to the front door jingled, signaling the arrival of a customer and saving me from responding. None of that was subtle. Another reason for Brad to not like Charli — she sees right through him. She surprises me by leaning her head back into the workroom and says that I have a visitor out front.

Immediately, I expect that it's Brad. Or it could be my mother. Or Jan. But I'm wrong on all counts. It's Jack Weller, looking charming and sheepish and outrageously handsome in an un-tucked blue button-down shirt, blue jeans and loafers. I'm blushing, I can feel the heat rising into my cheeks, but Charli pretends not to notice, and if Jack sees it, he's kept on a good poker face, because he keeps smiling away.

"Hey, I — uh, sorry. I was next door, and um, Rosie said you were here and well, I couldn't not say hi. I hope that's okay?"

"Hey, yourself. Yeah, no, it's…" *totally a bad idea. A fucking insanely bad idea.* "… fine, totally fine."

Jack Weller and I make awkward conversation for a few minutes under the watchful eye of Charli, who suddenly decides she needs to rearrange the orders on the board. Twice. In order to make things slightly less weird, Jack says loudly that he needs to buy a bouquet for his sister's birthday dinner that evening. Way too much detail, Jack. Way too much. But I wrap his flowers, ring him out and send him off. About an hour after he leaves, Charli casually says,

"Funny, in all the years Rosie an' I been next door, I don't recall Jack Weller's ever stepped foot through my door."

"Oh, that can't be. I'm sure he's been in before."

"Nope. I'd remember. Know what else is funny? Jack Weller's sister owns a flower shop. In Colorado."

I'm about to say, 'she could be here visiting,' but Charli's already walked into the back room and has started up the leaf stripping machine, a loud dinosaur of a machine that discourages conversation. I join her without another word, and for the next forty-five minutes we cut, strip and bucket flowers.

As we finish up, the store's phone rings as my phone lights up with a message. It's Jan, offering to pick Kadee up from preschool so the kids can start their play date early and I'll meet them at her house when I'm done working. Timing couldn't be better. Charli has taken an order for a funeral, so I can stay to help and still have a couple hours to myself after.

I should text Brad and let him know, but frankly? I don't feel like it. Nor do I feel like answering his three consecutive, 'what are you doing now' texts. Bad choice. The bell above the door jingles again, followed by the too loud voice of Bradley Handler. He's supposed to be working late, so this is an unpleasant surprise.

"Well, well, well, look at my working girl. Hello, Charli. Keeping her busy I see."

His smile is as fake as that jolly tone. I can see the hard glint in his eyes, and I've no doubt Charli can hear it in his voice. Between the lines you're saying, 'you should be home working, not here' and 'busy doing stupid shit, that's what you've got her busy doing.'

But there's something else, something more in his expression. It's the, 'is there something you want to tell me, Liv' look. It reminds me of a television lawyer in a courtroom right before he reveals the damning evidence that puts the bad guy away for life. The raised eyebrows, the slight but patronizing smirk. I understand what it means. He wants a confession from me for something.

With him, it could be anything ranging from my failure to pick up the dry cleaning again to the fact that Jack Weller was standing right where he is less than two hours ago. But I'm not going to bite. Not here, not now, and especially not in front of Charli.

"Thought you were working late. What are you doing here, Brad?" I tried to sound at least neutral, since I couldn't fake being pleased, but of course, he has to make a thing of it.

"What, Liv? Aren't you happy to see your husband? Isn't this a nice surprise? Or did you already have a surprise visitor today, hmm?"

Fuck. He knows Jack Weller was here, and he's not going to come out and say it, instead he'll make me say it. So that means he's been lurking around here for at least two hours, waiting and watching for me do something wrong.

But, you know what, Bradley? Fuck you. I didn't do anything wrong. Today.

Meanwhile, Charli is covertly listening from the back room while appearing although she's not. There is a slanted mirror at the doorway where from the cash register and back counter, we can see one another, but the customers cannot.

"Lots of local people come through the shop, Bradley. They're all a surprise since I haven't seen most of them in years."

Two can play at this game. If he doesn't ask, I'm not going to tell. He starts walking around the shop, lifting knick-knacks and setting them down again, doing his version of a courtroom interrogation routine. The only thing giving me more anxiety than him, is worrying that Charli will say I can leave if I want, since we finished the bulk of the work. If she does, then I'll be stuck leaving with him, and he'll suggest we go get something to eat, or worse, home for sex.

"Mhhmmm. So no one special? No one in particular stopped by the shop today? I'm surprised, you'd think Kadee would want to visit mommy at work."

Now I'm confused. Kadee? What does Kadee have to do with anything? She's with Jan and Christian. Then I remember the last text from Jan, she was taking them to the new frozen yogurt place up the street which is next door to a golf store. Now *I'm* growing suspicious. Maybe he did see Jack Weller come in here, and maybe he didn't.

All the more reason not to falter. In fact, it's a perfect time to turn the tables.

"Well, since Kadee is having a play date, I'm sure frozen yogurt is more exciting than being here. Did you have a nice visit with her, or were you too busy in the golf store to say hello to your daughter?"

Ha, gotcha sucka.

I see him squirm, that's exactly what he did, the shady shit. He saw his child sitting in the yogurt shop, and instead of going in to say hello, he snuck off and went next door to the golf shop. Then, because he can't *not* spy on me, he came here, hoping to catch me doing something wrong. Well, I'm done with his game. He shrugs.

"Whatever. Looks like you're done for the day here. Or do you still have more *arrangements* to make?" The way he says 'arrangements' is the same way I would say 'charming' when referring to Bradley. Sarcastically, derisively, and condescendingly.

Before I can answer, Charli saves the day for me and 'coincidentally' pops her head around the corner and says, "Oh, Livvy — any chance you could stay a little longer? I have a large funeral order to work on and could really use your help. You don't mind, right Bradley?"

Now it's her turn for sarcasm. She says Bradley the same way he said 'arrangements.' He, with all his macho chauvinistic comments and bully behavior, can't come up with anything to say, other than, "Sure, sure. Not at all." His words are jovial, but I see his jaw clenching. He's pissed.

"So, are you off for the rest of the day, Bradley?" I ask innocently.

"No," through clenched teeth, "I'm going back on the road. Twelve offices to see. I just thought it would be nice to surprise my wife." He leans in close, smiling in case Charli can see, and says, "Is that why your fucking old bookstore boyfriend came by, to surprise you? Those flowers he bought better not have been for you. See you at home tonight, Liv."

He shouts out a cheerful, 'See ya, Charli' towards the back room, and with a sharp jingling of bells, he is out the door. I release the breath that I'd unconsciously been holding, loosen my grip on the pencil I'd been squeezing, and catch and hold Charli's eye in the mirror for a moment before straightening up the front register area.

I take extra care in restocking the vases, folding boxes, and organizing the bows by color. I'm not ready to face her, not ready to leave either. There's hardly any more work left to be done, at least not so much that she couldn't do it alone, she was helping me avoid my husband.

When there's nothing left to fix, stock or adjust, I walk into the back room. Charli puts down her knife when I do. She's been patiently waiting. At first, she sighs a couple times, deciding how to begin, what to say.

After a while, she says, "You know what I remember about your mom from when we were young?"

I shake my head.

"Your mom was always a 'pleaser' never stood up for herself, always kind of went along. She dated a string of conceited jerks. Football captain, soccer star... Joey Farelli. He was a drummer. Your mom had a thing for musicians for a while there. Anyhow, I used to say to her, 'Mo, why the hell do you put up with these guys? You can do better.' And your mom, with them big doe eyes, like you got, would just shrug. She never had an answer." Charli shook her head, then continued. "Right about the time she met your dad, we graduated and lost touch. Just like that. But through the years I heard things — small town, you know — and I heard when they'd split up."

Charli de-thorned a rose with a thoughtful expression on her face. I guess she's trying to decide what to say next. Or how to say it.

She continued. "Now, I have no idea what went on with your parents, what their relationship was like, but I do know something changed with Mo after that divorce. The woman you grew up with is very different from the one I grew up with back then."

Charli put down her knife and swiveled in her chair to face me. "The old Mo would never have gone for her real estate license and eventually become a broker with her own company. I guess what I'm trying to say to you, Livvy, is that life — real living — is about making hard choices sometimes, and making them for yourself, not to please others. I'm willing to bet that's what happened with your mom. She got tired of being treated like crap."

Wow. Two long speeches from Charli in one day. I never knew she and my mom had been friends in high school, she'd never mentioned Charli even once that I can recall. It makes sense now, Charli represents a time in life that she'd rather not revisit. There was no detectable trace of Mo Hauer that was friends with Charli LaPierre in Maureen Hauer Perry, Broker & Owner of M. H. Perry Real Estate.

Something tells me that Charli is as she always was, direct, unassuming and self-sufficient.

"I can't even imagine my mother dating, let alone being called Mo." I wasn't ignoring all the other things she said, or the message behind them, I just didn't know how to respond. She's right of course, in her not-so-subtle let me-help-you-read-between-the-lines kind of way.

If I want to get away from Bradley, it'll be up to me, and it's going to be hard. Am I strong enough? Am I ready? I barely have any money set aside, definitely not enough for a lawyer. Wow. That's the first time I allowed myself to think that far, that seriously about leaving. Until now, it's been fantasies of him leaving me, or him dying unexpectedly.

I'd never admit that out loud to anyone, especially to Bradley. But it's true. Sometimes I watch our street through the living room window when he's running late, and I think, what if he gets into an accident? I mean, I carry out that fantasy *far*. I'd have his life insurance policy, the house, and the cars. I could sell what we don't need, and Kadee and I could be happy and free. Then of course, I feel guilty. Poor Kadee would grow up without a father and always long for him because she'd build him up in her mind as being a mythical God instead of the guy who came home every night and complained about how many lights were on in the house and take his dinner into his man cave and ignore her.

I realize Charli is still looking at me, waiting for more. "Charli—I... thank you. I suppose you've gotten an eyeful and an earful these past few days. I'm sorry about today — all the nonsense. My life right now... well I'm figuring it all out. I'll totally understand if I'm more drama than I'm worth here and you want me to stop coming around."

That's the last thing I want to happen, but I'm also mortified by my current situation.

Charli smiles kindly and says, "Oh, please. This is better than my soaps. Now get yourself out of here for the day and do something nice for yourself. I'll see you and little Miss. Kadee on Wednesday."

We both laugh as I grab my stuff and head out the back door with a wave. I still have a couple hours before Jan is expecting me and I decide to take Charli's advice. Against my better judgment, I go next door to the bookstore, looking furtively about the lot as I do. I'm already in big enough trouble with Brad, so why not just say fuck it?

TWENTY-THREE *THE REST OF THE DAY*

1 P.M.

Today, big band era swing is playing scratchily from the phonograph and the dress form is now wearing a beaded gown and has the cardboard head of Rosemary Clooney peeking out from under a felt hat adorned with a cluster of ostrich feathers. A handful of customers mill about, some browsing and some taking up the cozy leather chairs and reading, which is exactly what I plan on doing after I say a quick hello to Rosie.

Only, instead of Rosie reading a book on homeopathic medicine — or something like that — it's Jack Weller smiling at me. *'Yay. Shit..'* Except it sounds like one word.

Yayshit. I also take a second, suspicious look at each of the patrons, making sure none of them are Brad.

I've got a believable enough story for why Jack came into the flower shop- one that is ninety-nine percent fact and one percent omission, but I could have no justification for going into a bookstore knowing my jealous, possessive husband's feelings on such an act of high treason.

I should turn around and walk right back out that door, get in my car and go home. But I don't. I'm feeling brave — *reckless* — and carefree, *stupid*, so I walk up to the counter and act like that long gone seventeen-year-old girl that Jack Weller had a midlife crisis over.

I'll spare the details. Let's say the flirtation level was high and the thought of Bradley Handler was low. Like nonexistent low. Jack Weller knows my work schedule better than Brad does now, which all out guarantees future flower shop visits. I'm aware that he still helps Rosie from time to time. Before I leave, I notice the vase of flowers I'd wrapped for him myself sitting on the counter behind him.

"You could've said they were for Rosie, silly."

"I know, I know. I froze. Livvy, I'm not good at pretending, or lying for that matter. Listen, you and I both feel there's something between us, and I think we need to figure this out, don't you?"

What he really means is that *I've* got to resolve this, whatever *'this'* even is. Right now, it's a flirtation that picked up right where it left off almost five years ago. Does it have the potential to be something more than that? Pros: He's older, established, handsome, charming, has kids. Cons: We have over a twenty-year age difference.

Oh, yeah, and I'm a married woman. Can't forget that detail, now can we? Don't get me wrong, I'd love to forget Brad ever existed, and instead imagine romantic walks on the beach or curling up in front of a fire with Jack Weller, or taking Kadee to the park, going to his kid's games, and living a simple happy life with a man who doesn't repulse me. Something that, until now, I'd resigned myself to never having. Jack Weller has awoken in me something I thought was long since squashed by my marriage, hope.

"Jack, I—"

"You're not happy, Livvy, and you have a right to be. I say you and I deserve a shot."

"It's not that simple, Jack. You know it isn't. I'm married."

"I realize that, I do. And the last thing I want to do is pressure you. But I do want you to consider it. Consider *us*. I'm not going anywhere, Liv. I'm a patient man. Hell, I've already waited five years for you."

At this, he smiles. I know perfectly well that he hasn't been waiting around for me, but it's sweet of him to say nonetheless. It isn't until I'm in my car driving to Jan's with a dopey grin on my face, that I suddenly allow Brad to cross my mind. No, he crashed into my brain like a fricking SWAT team busting down a door. Like a Storm Trooper. Like a jealous husband who's caught his wife cheating.

Anyhow, back to fear and loathing. Bradley knows that Jack was in the flower shop today. I replay the visit. Did we hug? No, thank God. Did he stay long? Not unreasonably so, for someone buying flowers. Oh, my God. Did I walk him to the door? Yes? No, no I didn't. Of course, I didn't.

Okay, so all he could've seen is that I smiled at Jack, and only if he were standing in the door — which he was not. So, in a nutshell, no big fucking deal. Except in his mind, of course. He's going to make it a very big fucking deal, because that's what he does. I resolve to worry about it later because right now I am going to have a lovely rest of the afternoon with Jan and the kids. And a glass of wine.

TWENTY-FOUR *WHEN IN DOUBT, NAP*

9:53 P.M.

Confession. I let Kadee take a nap on the way home from Jan's. In fact, I drove especially slowly to ensure that she would fall asleep. That little nap guaranteed she wouldn't be going to bed before midnight, and that I'd be staying in her room with her until she did. It also meant that I'd conveniently fall asleep as well and stay there all night. Thereby avoiding the confrontation Brad's been preparing all day long.

When I hear his car pull in the driveway, I can't help but smirk. I am actually childish and petty enough to think, '*haha, I win.*' Of course, all I've really won is a postponement of the inevitable. But, if I can put him off long enough to find something to turn the tables on him — find something for him to feel guilty about — I really will win this one.

I'm reading a story to Kadee when his shape darkens the doorway. My innocent, 'oh, hello' expression is met by an 'are you fucking kidding me' head shake.

"Hi Daddy. Me and Mommy are having a slumber party."

"Hey, Kadee-Bear. How about telling Mommy to have a slumber party with Daddy for once?"

"Nooo, Mommy stay here. Read, Mommy."

I shrug, he scowls and walks to the bedroom in a huff, muttering the customary 'Jesus-fucking-Christ' as he does, and Kadee and I resume the story.

JUNE

TWENTY-FIVE *AVOIDANCE*

11:30 A.M.

I'm becoming an expert in diversion tactics and evasion and somehow, I've managed to avoid talking, really talking to Bradley all week. I mean, we've seen each other, but it's either in passing as he leaves for work, or distraction loaded. I let Kadee have two sleepovers at our house, invited both our mothers for dinner, and hosted a jewelry party. He is pissed but hasn't had an opportunity to lay in to me, not even about Jack Weller. As much as I wish it, I'm sure he hasn't forgotten and is biding his time.

The arrival of the weekend, a time when most people are counting down for with excitement, brings a high level of dread. Bradley is off both Saturday and Sunday, and as of right now, there are no distractions planned. But I'm working on it. I have to keep him from sending Kadee off to his mother's for an overnight.

TWENTY-SIX *STUCK, OR NOT*

6:40 A.M.

I hear rain on the window panes, the roof. One peek at the weather forecast on my phone tells me there'll be no community garden today. We've no play dates scheduled. Neither of our parents is around. I've already done the grocery shopping. I have no excuses to get away from him, the house. Shit. At least I'll have a couple hours to myself if both he and Kadee sleep in. I'll make sure she is up before him, though.

I realize how shitty it is to use my child as a buffer, my blocker, from dealing with my husband. But I'm not ready. I don't know when, or how, or if I'll ever be. *I demand a divorce. I want a divorce.* It's so easy to say in my head.

Hell, I say it all the time. 'Brad, dinner's ready.' *I want a divorce.* 'No, Bradley, I'm too tired.' *I want a divorce.* 'Sure, dinner with your boss sounds fine.' *I want a divorce.*

I suppress a sigh and tip-toe downstairs, checking in on Kadee as I always do. Oh, to sleep so peacefully as does a child. Downstairs, quiet house. Nothing but the sound of the rain. I forgot to prep the coffee maker, so while I wait for it to brew, I daydream out the rain streaked kitchen window.

It's still just dark enough out that the street lamps are still on, and like a moment of Deja Vu, Jack Weller's now familiar figure passes under the glow of one of those lamps, jogging steadily toward our house

I resist the obviously insane urge to run out there and greet him. The middle of the night is one thing, early morning in the pouring rain is entirely another. Instead, I watch. His head is down. I start to wonder if perhaps he'll pass by the house without as much as a glance. But as he crosses through the pale beam of light beside the driveway — precisely where we stood that strange and surreal night not so long ago — Jack Weller stops and looks directly at the kitchen window. He sees me here. My silhouette is back lit by the dimmed kitchen light. We don't wave. I stand still with my empty cup in my hands, he with his hands on his hips, breathing heavily. I see his shoulders heave and the steam from his breath as it hits the cooler air.

It feels like time has stopped, but the click of the coffeemaker beside me tells me otherwise, blinks me from my trance. As if it was the signal of a spell being broken, Jack Weller begins jogging again and from the kitchen doorway, "You gonna stare out the window all day, or make some breakfast?"

My heart stalls and then kicks hard against my chest. I'm blocking the view, but still. Jesus. What the fuck is he doing up this early? If he sees me jump, he doesn't acknowledge it. He merely comes up beside me, pulls a cup from the cupboard and glances out the window with sleep bleary eyes. Jack Weller is nothing more than a shadow between lamp posts already and Brad says, "What kind of fucking idiot goes jogging in the rain? Eggs, scrambled. Bacon if you remembered to get it. None of that green shit you try to sneak in there, either.

I'm too shaky to argue. My voice will betray me, so I say nothing and pull out the frying pan and eggs, and the bacon that I did remember to get from the store, thank you very much. As I'm doing all of this, I can feel that I'm under his watchful eye as he noisily sips his coffee. I wrack my brain for why he'd be awake so early on a Saturday. It's not for work. At least I don't think so. Golf? No, rain would've canceled that. If I ask, he'll get pissed. I'll go with neutral conversation.

"Looks like rain all day."

"Yup."

"Kadee will want to go outside in her new rain boots, I'm sure."

"Yeah. Did you remember to pack a couple of lunches for me, or were you too busy with your new job?"

Lunches. Lunches. Think, damn it. Why does he want me to pack him lunches?

"Not yet, I wanted to check first what you wanted."

Wow, I'm getting good at this lying thing.

"Same thing I want every time I go with the guys to the races. What kind of dumb question is that? And they're going to be here in an hour, so get some presentable clothes on."

"Of course, Bradley, I know that. What do you think, I'll answer the door in my pajamas?"

"Dunno, I bet if you thought bookstore boyfriend was coming to the door, you would."

Ignore that. He's baiting, so just ignore it. He'll be gone within the hour.

Oh my God, I am beyond relieved. Defensive, but relieved. How did I forget that he was going to the races this weekend? Easy enough answer, I've been distracted. I'm practically euphoric as I make his artery clogging breakfast and his lunches for the road trip, thinking 'I'm free, I'm free, all weekend long, I'm free' that I don't hear his next question, until he repeats it a second time,

"Livvy, I said, are you happy?"

I'm so caught off-guard, so completely unprepared for this opportunity to lay it out there and say those four magic words, 'I want a divorce' that I blow it. Instead, I say, "What? Oh, Bradley, please. Yes. Eat your breakfast. I hear Kadee waking up."

Then I practically bolt out of the room. I did not hear Kadee waking up; I panicked, plain and simple. I had my moment, and I chickened out. If he is asking, then my guess is, he knows the answer. Deep down, he must. You're not a stupid man, Bradley. I've never mistaken you for that. But I guess I haven't given him due credit for being insightful or intuitive.

I may have bought myself the weekend, but this conversation is only beginning. And now that it is, I'm getting cold feet. Not, *'I've changed my mind and I don't want out'* cold feet, but *'I don't know how to do this, and I'm scared'* kind of cold feet.

I should talk to somebody, get a different perspective, but who? I'm not comfortable talking to anyone about all of this. Sure, Jan knows some. Barb knows some. Charli knows some. But no one knows the extent and depth of my unhappiness, the weight of my fear, my guilt, my loathing, the terrible thoughts I have about him, the inappropriate thoughts I have about Jack Weller. I don't think I can share that side of my life with anyone. They'll be disgusted by me. I'm disgusted by me.

I'm a coward who uses her daughter like a shield to avoid her husband (a guy who lives and breathes for his family, works hard, is an excellent provider, gives me everything and anything that I want, doesn't drink excessively or smoke) and who is having an emotional affair with another man. Who's the real bad guy here? Me. That's who.

If I were to put it down on paper, in black and white, it would say that basically, my biggest gripe in my life is that my husband is gross and vulgar, and a bit of a Neanderthal. He's not a bad guy; he's the product of his upbringing. A lot of women would love to be in the circumstances I'm in; being taken care of, not having to work, staying home to raise the kids. This is not a bad gig. So why don't I stop complaining and try harder? That's it. I will. I am going to accept Bradley as he is and try to make this work. I can do this. For Kadee's sake, I can do this. Now, I just have to avoid Jack Weller.

TWENTY-SEVEN *SUBMISSION*

8:20 P.M.

I've been psyching myself up for Brad's return tonight. I put in extra effort in cleaning the house, made his favorite meal, since he'll be hungry again by the time he gets here, and I will consent to sex tonight. I've even sent Kadee off to bed early. I am going to ignore the lewd comments, the rudeness, and his smell. I can do this. That is my new four-word mantra — I can do this.

So, when that door opens, and he greets my, "Hey, made you a late dinner. You hungry?" by belching the word yes, I smile blankly. Ignore it, ignore it, and ignore it.

214

Okay, got through that. Set the plate down, ask about the trip, offer him a beer. I don't overdo it or talk overly nicely because he'll get suspicious that I either want something or did something.

While he eats and talks — literally at the same time, but I ignore it — about his trip, I keep busy with cleaning up. So, I don't have to look at him. Stop those thoughts, I tell myself. And as he rubs his bloated stomach and kicks his shoes off under the table, saying, "So, am I gonna get some tonight, or what?"

I am able to respond in the affirmative without throwing a steak knife at his head. I even manage to say, "I'll turn down the sheets while you take your shower," instead of, *I hope you don't plan on touching me until after you've showered*, knowing that it's less antagonistic.

"Nah, I'll take a shower after we get it on. My luck Kadee'll wake up. Not taking the chance."

OhmyfuckingGod, you repulsive fucking animal. Nope, didn't say it. Suddenly, I realize this is a game he's playing here. He knows I've resigned myself to stay, and his flicker of fear and doubt on Friday night has done an about face. He feels as though he has the upper hand, got his power back, and now he wants to make sure I know it.

Once in the bedroom, he tells me to take off my clothes. All of them, he emphasizes. He knows I prefer to keep my night dress on but doesn't care. It's then that I smell the whiskey on his breath. Bradley is a beer guy, whiskey brings out something nastier in him than the usual piggishness. I've already agreed to have sex tonight, there's no backing out, and it's only more aggravation if I resist. I take the nightgown off, and because he thinks he's playing out some stupid porn video he likes to watch on his laptop — of course I know — he orders me to lie down on the bed.

"No, on your stomach. That's right. Reach down and touch yourself. I want to watch. Do it, Livvy."

This is not turning me on, it's making me sick. The only way I can get through this is by thinking of Jack Weller. I imagine it Jack's voice telling me to move my hand slowly, raise my ass up higher so he can see. I picture Jack's hands squeezing and kneading my ass, saying, that's right, just like that. It's the tip of Jack pressing against me, into me. Thrusting deeply as my hand moves faster, grabbing my hair and pulling, slapping and squeezing my ass. For the first time in years I allow myself release.

Immediately after, I feel disgusted and want it to be over. Thanks to the whiskey (I mean that sarcastically) it takes him a while to finish, so I lay there with my face in the pillow and wait. When he finally rolls off of me I get up quickly and go straight to the shower. If I stay in there long enough, he'll pass out.

As the hot water hits my back, I renege on every promise I made myself this weekend. I can't. I can't fucking do this for the rest of my life. Part of me wants to cry, deep down, I am, but I'm numb and cold and done. So fucking done.

JULY

TWENTY-EIGHT *YEAH, RIGHT*

10:30 A.M.

Of course, I'm not done. I'm still going through the motions, still pretending to the world and myself that everything is fine. Despite my ever-increasing revulsion at the thought of his touch. Despite that he's as persistent as ever, his memory of that night from a month ago is fonder than mine, he's still referring to it. I could vomit.

"Hey, how about a repeat of that other night? That was some good lovin' wasn't it?"

He has no idea what thoughts were in my head to get me through that degrading act. 'Good lovin.' Who even says that besides Barry White? In the 1970s. Anyhow, he agreed to let me put Kadee in summer session preschool for four days a week instead of three, thanks to that night. She's been asking to 'go more school' and it helps me out as well, so today, I'm in the flower shop Sans kid.

Charli and I are working at a steady pace, she with one eye on her soap opera, me with my mind on my own. How many times have I flip-flopped on whether I can stay in this marriage? A dozen? A thousand? That would be more like it. A thousand at least. I have two arguments, Argument A. I do not want Kadee to be a statistic, a child of divorce like me. It's not her fault I was young and naïve — gullible, immature, and stupid — so she shouldn't have to pay for my bad decisions any more than she already does. Basically, I made my bed, so I should have to lie in it. Argument B. I don't want Kadee growing up seeing her mother and father in a loveless marriage. That's no example for a child. Nor do I want her to think that the way her father treats her mother is normal.

So, the question is, which of those two choices is the lesser of the evils? The answer is... I don't know. I just don't. As if on cue, from the flat screen TV, Chad dramatically says to Lacy — yes, I've learned all the characters names now — "Lacy, my love, sometimes you just need to close your eyes and jump."

Then Lacy, equally dramatic, "But, Chad, I'm afraid. What will I do? Where will I go?"

Ah, soap operas.

"Don't worry, Lacy. I have a yacht. Sail away with me, and I'll take care of you."

Wow, soaps are still selling old style fairy tales, huh? Why not, 'We're all afraid, Lacy. Life is scary, but you can do it on your own, I have faith in you,' instead? Probably because that would make it not a soap opera.

Damn, that makes me angry. That's the crap I grew up on, believing those not so subliminal messages, women were damsels in distress and in need of a prince to save them. *I* had wanted a prince, and instead I got Bradley. He swept me up with gifts and promises, away from my mother who wanted me to take the real estate exam and join her company, away from my dreams of California and acting. And I let him because I was too chicken to follow my dreams and too stubborn to follow my mother.

So what am I weighing here? Safety and security coupled with indebtedness and misery, or the great unknown coupled with figuring it out for myself, by myself. This sucks, this not knowing what to do. If I'm to be honest with myself, I've always taken the easy route. Path of least resistance, quick fixes, shortcuts. I've spent so much time avoiding conflict and controversy that I'm a watered down, vanilla version of myself. I want *me* back, damn it. But I'm scared.

"Um, everything okay over there? That arrangement is so tight, it looks like a ball."

I step back from the flowers and realize she's right. I've been putting all of my tension into the arrangement, and it shows.

"Sorry, guess I'm distracted. I'll fix it, don't worry."

"Not worried at all, it happens. Soap's about done if ya want to talk about what's eatin' you."

In the short time I've been working for Charli, I've come to understand that she is not one for empty words. She says what she means and means what she says. I'm not sure I'm ready to talk about Bradley, or Jack Weller for that matter, but I am curious about her.

"How long were you married for, Charli?"

"Twenty-seven years, till the cancer took him. Would've been thirty-seven this June."

"Were you happy? Happily married, I mean."

"Oh, sure. We had our ups and downs like anyone else. It wasn't easy starting the business, took us a while to build a clientele but we managed. There were a lot of macaroni dinners and peanut butter and jelly lunches back in those days, let me tell you."

She is smiling, a wistful expression on her face. I can easily remember the condo Brad and I rented when we first married. Brad's parents helped us with the security and first and last, my mother found the place and gave us her old living room set. I liked it well enough, but he hated it.

He didn't like the neighborhood or the neighbors, especially the single guy that lived next door. As soon as he landed the westerly district, which meant a big income increase, he put a deposit on the house. Sight unseen, and without asking my opinion. He assumed I'd be thrilled and grateful, I assumed that was how I was supposed to feel.

"You still miss him, huh?"

"I do. We were best friends, did everything together. We were supposed to be doing this together until we were ready to retire. But, life is what happens while you're busy making other plans, isn't it?"

"I'm really sorry, Charli. That's so sad."

"Sad? No, not at all. We were lucky, I am lucky. Some people go through their whole lives not knowing that kind of love. Now that is sad. Imagine that, spending all your days without love? Hmph. I'd rather be alone."

Another of Charli's skills, euphemisms. Since she's opened the door, I decide to step through it, slowly.

"So, what if you'd been unhappy with your husband? Would you have stayed with him, or left him and risk losing the business and everything you have?"

Charli taps the point of her knife on the scarred counter a few times, thinking. No doubt she's deciding whether to continue with the euphemisms or talk straight. She sets her knife down and turns fully to me. Here it comes.

"Well, Livvy, there are different levels and kinds of unhappy, aren't there? There's the kind where, say, money is tight and you're both stressed out, not knowing what's next so you get a little testy with each other. Hell, even have some big fights, but then realize you're better and stronger together than apart. That's the temporary kind, comes and goes."

Charli looks at me to see if I'm following, so I nod, and she carries on. "Then there's the kind that is all wrong, with little chance of every truly being right. Incompatible, unrelatable, and thoroughly unpleasant. Sure, you can stay there, in that kind of unhappy, but it'll never go away. I've had the first kind of unhappy, and I'd say you've got the second.

So, if you're asking me if I could stay married in the second kind, I'd have to say no, I would not. But I'm not you, Liv, and I can't tell you what to do. I suspect that if and when you get good and tired enough, you'll make your move."

That morning, Charli began the weekly project of teaching me all about the business end of operating a flower shop. How to order from growers, the computer system, and the different national floral organizations. Every conversation came with a lesson and an explanation about floral design, marketing, tools, and wholesalers. I was learning a trade and loving it.

NOVEMBER

TWENTY-NINE *WINDS OF CHANGE*

11:01 A.M.

"So, explain it to me again. Why is it that you suddenly have to work on a Saturday? I thought you said this little 'job' of yours wasn't going to interfere with home life. It's interfering, so what the fuck?"

"Actually, no, I'm not going to explain it again. I've already explained it, three times as a matter of fact. Perhaps you can explain to *me* what part of *Charli needs my help on Saturdays this month and next month, and I said yes* is so difficult to grasp?"

"Well, I told *you*—I'm not babysitting."

"Well, Bradley, if by 'babysitting' you mean that you will not co-parent the child you co-created, that's fine. I've already made arrangements with Jan. Kadee and Christian will have play dates on Saturdays at Jan's, and on Thursday nights we will have play dates here while Jan takes a night class."

His mouth opens, closes.

What's wrong, Bradley? You seem dumbstruck. Is it because I've already figured out every argument you could have? Or that I'm not backing down? That's been happening a lot lately, hasn't it?

I imagine a miniature Charli and Jan sitting on my shoulder, cheering me on, while on the other shoulder a frowning disproving Rita. Screw you, Rita. And screw you, too, Brad. I can call his next move before he even opens his mouth. He's about to go with the old fall back, 'Sorry for wanting to spend time with my wife' line. Too bad I've walked away and before he could drop it.

"Kadeeeee, come on down and say bye to Daddy. Time to go play with Christian."

Kadee comes down the stairs with squeals of excitement and boundless energy. Now he really can't say no. Not that I'd listen anyhow. We're out the door and singing along to Disney Radio the whole ride before he's picked his jaw up off the floor. Both Mommy and daughter are in excellent spirits, thanks to this Indian summer we're having. Oh, and the fact that we are free of him for the day. That helps, it really does. Every day is one step closer to being truly free of Bradley Handler. Well, I guess I'll never really be totally free of him, but I won't be married to him. And that is pretty damn liberating.

He, of course, is suspicious. My newfound feistiness makes him wary but since I occasionally submit to him climbing and grunting on top of me like a gorilla, he says little. We take turns playing offense and defense, we resemble a human chess match. I'm not sure how much longer I can go on like this, yet I'm still not quite ready to make the move. I debate daily on how, on when.

I imagine us sitting at a table in a quiet restaurant, some place where he'll be forced to keep his cool, and I'll say, *'Bradley, I'm sure you must realize that things have not been good between us for some time, and well, I want a divorce.'* Or, *'Bradley, you and I both know this isn't working. I think we should get a divorce.'* Not very creative, but to the point. When I'm feeling really snarky, I come up with sentences like, *'You are the most repugnant, knuckle dragging, Cro-Magnon, vile human I have ever known. I am leaving you, you disgusting pig.'*

Okay, so that last one may be more vicious and hateful than snarky, I agree. Of course, I also imagine all sorts of responses from him, and none of them involve him saying, *'Oh, okay. You can have the kid and the house, I'll just pack my stuff and go.'* It's the reality of it all that gives me cold feet. This isn't Charli's soap opera, this is real life, and he is going to go off the wall. I know this. I know it as sure as my own name. Which I'll be taking back, by the way, Bradley. Oh, but I'll have a different last name than Kadee. Sigh. Is any part of this going to be easy? Stupid question. It won't.

A few minutes and four choruses of 'Five Little Monkeys' later and we are at Jan's. She smirks knowingly at my cheerful demeanor. We've been talking about my 'situation.'

That's you, Bradley. You're my situation.

I've stopped hiding like a scared rabbit, stopped burying everything like a dirty secret. At first, I was embarrassed and ashamed. I should add guilty to the list, I should feel guilty, but I don't. I'm too angry, too bitter. Too right.

"Hey there, you two. How goes it? Kadee, you run on inside, Christian is watching something mind numbing on TV, you can go get brain dead with him."

"Yay. Thanks Miss. Jan. Bye, Mommy, have fun making flowers, I'm gonna give Christian my Velociraptor picture and get brain dead."

"Bye, honey. Love you." To Jan, laughing, "Brain dead? Really, Jan?"

We both laugh. If that's the worst Kadee says after having Bradley as a father, we're lucky.

"So, I'm guessing by that look on your face that everything went well this morning with Mr. Sunshine? Don't tell me he was actually fine with you working weekends now? Oh, God, don't tell me Hot DCD is back in town?"

"Ha. Yeah right. And no, I mean, not that I know of. Anyhow, I didn't back down, and I didn't give him a chance to stop me."

It's unnecessary to mention that Jack Weller returns from Atlanta today. Fine, I admit it. Jack Weller is part of why I'm in such a good mood, as well as why I'm excited about weekends at Charli's. It is easier to see Jack that way. There, I said it. It's been confirmed repeatedly, I am as shitty a person as Brad is, just in a different way. I do get to claim one caveat. Jack Weller and I are not having an affair. Not a physical one, at least. And, yes, in my book it still counts. I haven't forgotten that I'm supposed to feel guilty. But Brad's after work trips to the strip club really erase that guilt quite nicely.

"Good for you, kiddo. Keep it up. And stay away from the hot DCD. See ya later, no rush. We're making DIY pizzas later. Should be a disaster, but whatever."

I wave off her warning and laugh as I hop back in the car. These days only Jan could say something that resembles an order and not get her head bit off for it. She's right of course. Even being seen talking with Jack is asking for trouble. Yet, today, after I finish work at the flower shop, I am heading over to First Congregational to prep the community garden for winter and Jack Weller is going to help me do it. No one needs to know that, least of all, Brad Handler.

THIRTY *FIRST CONGREGATIONAL, AGAIN*

3:45 P.M.

Charli mostly leaves me to do much of the work on my own now, trusting that I have learned enough these past months to handle it without any concern on her part. At first, I was resistant. I didn't want that kind of responsibility, but she put the keys in my hand and said, 'You'll be fine. Any problems call me. I'll be at the beach.' She wasn't kidding, either. She left me in charge of the shop on a sunny Wednesday morning and I didn't see her until the next day. However, today we work together, both of us have reasons to get our work done and leave early, neither mentioned the respective reasons behind the rush.

When I pull into the church lot, I see Jack Weller's SUV is already there, and he's leaning against his hood, arms crossed, and staring out over the garden, until I pull in, that is. I see the smile that lights up his face, and mine matches.

Though I want to jump out and run to him, I show restraint. Slowly opening the car door, stepping out and letting my long hair drape in front of my face. As I look up at him, I tuck the loose hair behind my ear and smile, suddenly shy. It's been almost two months since we've seen each other.

The Atlanta job had come unexpectedly, requiring him take week long and sometimes even longer trips to oversee the job. It has kept the development of 'something more' at bay, and to be honest, it's therefore a bit of a Godsend. Temptation removed, I can focus on what needs to be done instead of what I want to do.

Point proven, because instead of all the things I should be doing right now, I am here, in a church parking lot, making puppy eyes at Jack Fricking Weller. His time under the Atlanta sun has preserved his summer tan, and of course, his white cotton t-shirt accentuates it as well as his perfectly white teeth. I blush as I imagine those teeth biting into my shoulder while we make love on the hood of his car.

Whoa, that came out of nowhere. I could quite literally fill a porn book with all the erotic fantasies I have of this man.

Know what I could fill up with fantasies about you, Bradley? An arrest warrant.

Kidding. Kidding. Sort of. I'd never leave Kadee parentless, geesh.

"Hey, you."

"Hey. So, your email said you got in late last night, huh? You must be exhausted."

"I did, I was. Till I saw you that is. Any way we could sneak a quick hug here?"

Considering what was in my head a second ago, it's not the craziest request. I mean, it *is* crazy, just not by comparison. So, like a fugitive, I give the lot, church and street a furtive scan. No cars, no people, no Brad. I walk into Jack Weller's arms like I'm walking to Jesus. I know that's blasphemous, especially while standing in a church parking lot, but saying, 'like walking in to home' is not a good analogy right now. Someday it will be, but not right now. And anyhow, this hug? Well, he hugs me like I am his long-lost lovey from childhood, his treasured gift, his salvation. Tenderly, tightly, fully. Though it'd be impossible, it feels like our entire bodies touch in that brief hug.

Brad and I don't hug. Ever. He never was one for hugs, or hand holding. I forget how love and affection starved I am until I am around Jack Weller. Actually, before Jack came back into my life that fateful May day, I was repulsed by the idea of being touched. Not even just by Brad, by anyone. I couldn't even imagine wanting a man, he'd turned me off that much. But look at me now. Willing to commit adultery. My, I've grown so much. Listen, I realize this is fucked up. I do. My justifying it by telling myself how awful my husband is, is not making it any more right.

But I'm leaving you Bradley. I am fucking leaving you. You just don't know it yet.

And I have the next two hours to be in under the fading fall sunshine with Jack Weller, tucked partially away behind the church, far enough from the road that we could be anyone at all, so I am taking it. We will turn the soil, rake and clear debris, and laugh and talk, and yes, flirt, until it is time to go our separate ways. Two streets apart from one another.

THIRTY-ONE *SNEAKY BASTARD*

9:28 A.M.

I am furious. Shaking, heart-pounding, fist-clenching furious.

You fucking fucker.

I woke up this morning, and like I often do after he's left, I check my top-secret email account for messages. There are two senders from which I receive mail. Jack Weller and my hidden bank account. There is only one message, and it's from the bank, sending an electronic receipt for withdrawal. Account Balance: $0.39. No need to contact the bank, It was Brad. He discovered my secret fund. I don't know how he found out, but I'll guess he snooped better than I hid. There was almost five thousand dollars in there, more than enough for a retainer for a lawyer plus some 'cushion', and now it's gone.

Here comes the cat-and-mouse game. If I deny him the money, he'll take it anyway and it'll be a huge fight. If I give it over and try to say it was meant for a surprise, he'll take it anyway. Either way, my money is gone, and I am fucked. I want to cry and scream and throw things and fucking kill him. But Kadee is waiting for breakfast, grocery shopping needs to be done, and I will have to pretend like everything is fine.

As hard as I try, I'm still transparent enough for Kadee to see through. Twice she has asked, 'what's wrong, Mommy' and I have smiled brightly and told her everything is fine, just fine. If I use that word one more time, I'll scream. She's a smart little girl, and though she seems to take my assurance at face value, I feel her watching me surreptitiously as she colors in what appears to be a Pteranodon.

She and Christian exchange drawings almost daily now. Dinosaurs for him, flowers, dragonflies and birds for her. It's extremely sweet, and Jan and I have decided to keep their artwork and turn them into keepsake books for when they are older. At this rate, the books may be the thickness of War and Peace.

Thinking of War and Peace, I need to figure this out before I talk to Bradley. Normally, he would have texted already with a list of grocery store wants, or reminders to do one thing or another, but he is suspiciously silent.

Waiting, that's what he's doing. Waiting for me to make the first move here. Well, guess what?

You're going to have to keep waiting because I haven't figured out what the fuck I'm going to say, Bradley, you shit. Or do, for that matter.

I close the refrigerator door harder than what's necessary, making Kadee jump. Damn it. Poor kid. I decide to put off the problem and focus on her. I refuse to ruin our Mommy/daughter day. Between me working and Kadee going to school all day now, we don't get these special times as much as we used to. Fortunately, it's a teacher in-service day, so no school, and I am off as well. So, first stop grocery store, then children's museum.

For the sake of saving time, I opt for the closer grocery chain rather than the natural foods store, and as we round the corner of organics into health and beauty, we run smack into none other than Jack Weller. We are both too stunned to say anything at first.

Kadee says, "Mommy, mind your manners."

We both burst out laughing. Jack knows not to introduce himself. I of course offer no introduction. Just two strangers colliding in a grocery aisle, happens all the time.

"Ah, not at all little Miss., it was my fault. So sorry ladies, I hope no one is injured?"

"We are perfectly fine, thank you, sir. You are well also?"

"Oh, yes, yes. Although, I may have a case of whiplash... perhaps we should exchange numbers and insurance info?"

Well, we are cracking ourselves up here in the middle of the very popular grocery store, aren't we? Wouldn't you know it, the obvious happens. Rita rounds the corner. At the sight of us — no doubt looking more like a happy family than strangers who'd just bumped carts. She raises her pencil drawn eyebrows in surprised disapproval. Of all fucking people. You're kidding me, right?

Wordlessly she looks from me to Jack Weller, giving him the full examination. Her weasel eyes start at his thick, tousled hair, right down to his work boot clad toe. Saying nothing to Jack, her sharp gaze turns back to me. She is behind Jack, so while he does not see her, he sees my frozen expression and quickly jumps into action. Loudly, he says, "Well, ladies, again, so sorry for smashing into your cart. Hope the rest of your shopping goes safely," and walks away, without even glancing at Rita.

As I begin to release the breath I was holding, Kadee calls out, "Wait. Don't you still want our number?"

The exhale becomes a sharp inhale, Jack keeps walking, as if he didn't hear her, and I'm helplessly shrugging at the now red-faced Rita. No matter how I explain this, she will still go right back to her son with the story of how a handsome man was talking to his wife in the grocery store and trying to get her phone number. I try anyway.

"Well, that sounded wrong. Ha, ha. He was, uh, making a joke... whiplash, lawyer, you know... yeah, anyhow. Hello Rita, grocery shopping, are you?"

"No, I'm getting my tires rotated. Yes, obviously I'm grocery shopping, Olivia." To Kadee, and in a sickly sweet baby tone, "Hello my little darling. Was that fresh man trying to talk to your Mommy?"

Before Kadee can answer, my anger gets the best of me and I respond sharply. Something I've never done before. The look on her face, oh, it is priceless. "Rita, I told you what happened here, so I'd appreciate you not putting such ideas in her head, thank you."

"What, well I—"

"I know exactly what you meant. It was inappropriate."

Silence. Except for Rick Astley on the stores speakers that is. Blink. Blink. Blink.

"Well, I was just—"

"Teasing, yes, I'm sure. Anyhow, I'd love to chat, but Kadee and I have big plans today, don't we Kadee-bear?"

"Grandma, we're going to the museum today."

Rita, with two scarlet dots on her cheeks turns her attention to Kadee, and they discuss what she'll see and do there as I silently fume. And gloat, and almost laugh. Jack has passed by the aisle twice now, feigning nonchalance and affecting the air of a customer trying to find an elusive item on his grocery list.

After a long minute, we part ways both with forced friendliness. The minute she turns the corner, she'll be calling Bradley. I'm certain. Only now, her focus will be more on how mean and rude I was to her rather than the particularly handsome man trying to pick up his wife. At least, that's my hope.

Kadee and I have a lovely day, almost perfect were Brad and my stolen money not so heavily on my mind. He still has not called or texted, and neither have I. If we keep circling the ring like this, we're gonna get booed out of the arena, Bradley. What's his angle going to be? What's mine going to be, for that matter? I play out numerous scenarios in my mind, laying out every foreseeable outcome. I keep trying to calm down, but the more I think about everything, I'm getting angrier and angrier.

All the sneaky shit he does behind my back. The strip clubs, the casino nights, the golf clubs, all of it. When he goes through my purse at night — when he thinks I'm sleeping — I know. When he logs on to my laptop, checks my non-secret emails, I know. My only question is how he found my very secret account information.

There are three spots I log in from. Work, the public library, and my cell phone. I always, always clear my browsing history and cached files. No cookies. Nothing is saved, ever. I leave my checks and banking paperwork at the flower shop, tear up my deposit slips and... my deposit slips.

Wait. Saturday, after work, I deposited money. What did I do with the slip? Think, damn it, think. I used the machine so that I wouldn't have to speak to a teller. My phone rang. It was my mother, a lengthy discussion about a house on Westerly that she was trying to find a buyer for.

Then that asshole in the Prius cut me off and I had to slam on my brakes. All my shit flew off the passenger seat onto the floor of the car. Change, money, make-up, everything spilled out. Son of a bitch. The bank card was in that jumbled mess and I never stopped back at Charli's to place it back in the lock box that she bought especially for me. It wasn't the deposit slip I'd forgotten about; it was the God damn bank card. I need to find out for certain.

Instead of going straight home from the museum, we make a pit stop at the flower shop. I have a set of keys, but text Charli to let her know, anyway. While Kadee looks around at all the flowers, I unlock the safe and see what I already suspect to be the case, the bank card is not there. Nor is it anywhere in my purse or the car. It is in Bradley's wallet, in his back pocket. I'm close to tears, but for Kadee's sake I pull it together and we drive home.

It isn't until Kadee has been in her bed napping soundly that I decide it is time to call Brad. Technically, he was the first to cave in and call. Four times in the past hour but left no messages. I fucking hate you, Bradley. And now I am trapped for even longer. No money, no lawyer, no escape. You win again. I am, in this very moment, resigned to it all. I'm tired and done and just fucking quit. I'm not cut out for the games and espionage and deceit, I tried it and I suck at it.

As I raise the phone up to call, it rings. Brad, of course. My ringtone is the old fashioned 'brriiiinnngg, briiiinnnng' sound and halfway through the third, I answer.

"Hey."

"I called you, like, two times. Whatcha doin'?"

"Four times, actually. Not including this call, Bradley."

"Whatever. So, what have you two been doing all day? Anything special?"

Really? Really, you fucker?

He knows exactly what we've been doing all day — what *I've* been doing all day. And just like that, I trade my resignation back in for rage. "Well, Brad, I don't know. Are you asking what we did before or after running into your mother at the grocery store? Or before or after the museum that I told you we were going to today? Or before or after I realized you went into my personal bank account? Which one, Brad?"

"What? Whatcha talkin' about Liv? *Personal* bank account? The only bank accounts you have are ones we have. You get how it works, don't you? What's yours is mine, and what's mine is... well, mine too, actually. That's a nice little sum of money you had set aside there, Liv. Now, what were you planning on doing with that money, hmm? How about a nice cruise for us? Oh, I know. A surprise gift for me for being such a great husband, right? You remember, the guy who does everything for you, gives you anything you want, and provides you a beautiful home, your own car..."

"Oh, cut the bullshit Bradley. For years you've been snooping in my purse, my computer, my car, you call ten thousand times a day, you question every single move I make, you didn't want me to get a job. You have never, ever trusted me, and I have never given you a reason. I'm sick of it. You hear me? I am so sick and fucking tired of your shit, Bradley. If you don't trust me, we shouldn't be married. I'm done. I'm so fucking *done* with this. I want a divorce."

Oh, my God. Oh, my God. Oh my *God*. I said it. Out loud. I told him I want a divorce. I feel like the world's largest balloon just popped, BOOM, followed by a rush of air, then deafening silence. Almost at once, the vacuum starts.

"Olivia, calm down. You're talking crazy. You—"

No turning back, the ball has begun to roll. My God, I have no money and I've dropped the hammer. I don't care. I can't — I won't turn back now.

"No. I don't want to hear it, Bradley. You've pushed me too far. I think you should stay at your parent's tonight. Kadee and I will be at Jan's when you get home. Text me when you leave the house."

I am prepared for him to tell me that I can get the fuck out of the house. I know how to respond.

You see, Bradley, I've done some self educating over the past few months.

I have more rights than what he wanted me to believe. Quite a lot more as it turns out. In fact, I hold the upper hand. But *he* always knew that, didn't he? He figured that if I was always dependent and scared to leave that I never would. Well, he was right… until now. I may have lost my attorney's retainer, but I have gained the knowledge that because of Kadee, I can stay in our house.

"Fine. Since you're acting like a crazy bitch, I'll go to my mother's until you calm the fuck down."

I say nothing more than an acknowledgement and hang up. I am shaking violently, shocked, terrified, outright giddy. My first thought is to call Jack Weller, which of course is a terrible idea that I resist. Jan? Yes, I'll call Jan and tell her we need to come over for a while. I think I'm not going to tell her anything, not just yet, at least, but the second she hears my voice, she knows something is up.

"What's wrong? That asshole do something?"

"No, God, no. I'm fine, really. I just — it's… I did it Jan. I told him."

"Oh, my fucking God. About Hot DCD?"

"Jesus, no. Are you crazy? And there's nothing to tell there. Not really, I mean. No, I told him I want a divorce and — ugh. I'll tell you the whole story when we get there. Kadee doesn't know anything. Pour wine, we'll be there in an hour."

My mind is racing, and yet I'm frozen at the kitchen table. Jesus, what to do I do with myself? I'm still shaking, now with nervous energy. Suddenly, it hits me, *the safe*. I need to get into that safe and clear out whatever he has of value in there. Tit for tat as they say. Please, God, have something of value in there. Cash preferably.

I run into the den, fearful and anxious that he'll arrive home sooner than later, assuming he'll stop by to pick up some things. Or confront me in person. The only saving grace is that he is more than halfway across the state today. It's only 2:30 now. Even if he drove ninety miles per hour, he couldn't get home before five o'clock, later with traffic. But still, my mind screams, 'hurry, hurry.'

My hands shake so much that I have to retry the combination three times. Finally, on the fourth attempt, I match the numbers up with the lines just right and pull. Nothing happens. Again, I try. Finally, I accept that fact that he changed the combination. Think, Livvy, think. What would he use? I almost laugh when it comes to me.

You, shit, you.

I bet he used the same pin number I used for my bank card. I try it, my birthday month and day. 1-1-23. Click. He thought I wouldn't try that? Damn, Bradley, you are no more original than I am. All the usual stuff in here, deed to house, titles to cars, life insurance, banking info. It dawns on me to take pictures of everything. Thanks to my friends and the internet, I'm a lot smarter than I used to be.

I also find several credit cards with their activation stickers still attached, most in my name. Those may be useful. Unfortunately, there is not nearly as much cash as I'd hoped, but a thousand dollars is better than nothing. There's my partial retainer. Guess what Bradley? What's yours is mine, too. I take it all.

Just as I close the safe, I hear Kadee come down the stairs. Acting as if all is wonderful, I tell her we have one more fun surprise for the day. We're going to have a play date with Christian. I wait impatiently as she draws him a Pterodactyl, she cannot leave until it's perfect. I eye the clock, driveway and my phone with mounting anxiety. I do not want to be here when he gets home. At the same time, I'm not sure if leaving the house is such a smart idea. What if he locks me, us out? What if he claims that I left him and somehow plays victim?

PART TWO
ONE YEAR, SEVEN MONTHS LATER
JUNE

THIRTY-TWO *A NEW LIFE*

9:58 A.M

I love summer. Well, and spring, and fall. I love everything these days. The garden is huge, twice the size of my first garden. Was that two years ago, already? Hard to believe how much can change in such a short amount of time. I smile over at Kadee as she rolls in the grass with Cowboy. The playful puppy nips and yaps as he prances and pounces on the giggling girl. From the house float the upbeat thump of teen pop music from an open upstairs window. My heart is bursting with happiness. From the house I hear, "Hey, you two. How about coming in for a snack? I sliced some fruit and made smoothies."

Kadee says, "No thanks. Me and Cowboy are busy."

I call out, "Sure, honey, give me five minutes, and I'll be in."

Oh, Kadee, honey.

I want to tell her to give him a chance, but I don't want to push either. So many changes in such a short time. She never seems angry, never act out. Her first-grade teacher said she's a joy to have in class. Her soccer coach says she is a great team player. But I worry. Those first months of the divorce were hard. And ugly. I tried to shield her as much as possible, really I did. Her father played dirty, like I knew he would. Not that'd I'd ever say that to her.

For months and months, we battled. I lost fourteen pounds that I couldn't afford to lose, even Bradley lost weight. The 'divorce diet' they call it. It wasn't as bad as I thought it'd be. It was worse. But after what seemed like an eternity, something changed and brought him to his senses, it would seem.

We're actually pretty good now. Not great, not friends, but not exactly enemies anymore. I'd never have predicted that. Not in a million years. But for Kadee, we try. And every day, it gets a little easier. I think the proof is in how she's adapted to this new life. I guess only time will tell. I ask, "Honey, you sure you don't want anything?"

"I'm sure, Mommy. Maybe some strawberries though. And a banana. Could I eat them out here?"

Hmm. Passive resistance. I recognize that tactic. She'll take the food from me, but not from him. Or I'm over-thinking it. Maybe she's changed her mind. Sigh. Maybe I should just relax and let things develop.

Everyone who dared say anything (Jan, Charli) warned me of the pitfalls of bringing someone new into Kadee's life so soon after splitting with her father. But, admittedly, I was selfish. I'm in love, for the first time in my adult life, I am in love. Speaking of love — I do so love watching her with that dog. Granted, it was a divorce guilt gift, but it's the one thing she'd asked for since she was two years old. Bradley and I never got around to it while we were married. So how could I not? Cowboy is a rescue dog, so I justify adopting him on all levels. Besides, it's nothing compared to the gifts her father lavishes her with every time he sees her. I sigh as I stand, giving Kadee a smile as I head to the house.

"Hey, beautiful, I was beginning to think you weren't coming in. I made this one especially for you. Kale, broccoli sprouts, pineapple and mango. Enjoy."

"Aww, Jack. You are so thoughtful. Thank you, honey. And, by the way, it's only been five minutes since you came out, silly."

I cannot believe how attentive Jack is. Or that he knows his way around a kitchen. Bradley never made anything but a mess in our old kitchen. In fact, Jack Weller more than knows his way around a kitchen; he custom designed this one for us to work in together.

Eight-foot kitchen island, restaurant sized refrigerator, top of the line appliances including the best rated juicer and food processor on the market. Not because he expects something from me, but because he shares my passion for cooking and enjoys our time together.

Macy bounces into the kitchen, steals a few strawberries and tells me the latest social media feud she is engaged it. At least she seemed to be thrilled at the relationship between her father and I. Becoming a step-mother-ish figure wasn't so hard, so far. In fact, it was

Macy's idea that we move in with them. Although her reasoning, 'so Dad will bother you all the time instead of me,' wasn't necessarily the most altruistic, it still tipped the scales.

The ink on the divorce papers had only been dry for three months before Kadee and I moved into Jack's house on Barnett. He was originally going to let his lease run out and buy a condominium, but for both Kadee's and my sake, he made an offer on the house and the owners accepted. It kept us in our neighborhood, and Kadee was able to play with the same neighborhood kids and stay in the same school. Two things I'd never been able to afford on my own.

Though I could have rightfully kept the house on Marshall, it was neither practical nor economical for me to do so. The market had dropped, so the value of the house decreased and by the time we were done with the lawyer's fees and debt payoffs we barely broke even. Turns out we were living beyond our means, a fact I was oblivious of. I spent a lot of time blaming Bradley for that, but once it dawned on me that was equally at fault, that my willful oblivion was as bad as his secrecy, I became determined to educate myself financially, and not repeat the same mistakes again.

I can promise you this much, Kadee, I will not let you be as clueless about money as I was.

THIRTY-THREE *NEW PLAN*

12:30 P.M.

"Well, what kind of flowers did you have for your first wedding?"

"Ugh, they were yellow and white. I hate yellow and white. And there were carnations. So not one single carnation, please. Or rose. Or baby's breath. Sorry, Charli. Those memories still irritate me. I let Bradley and his mother run the whole show, nothing was of my choosing. Thank God Jack is so easy going. All he said was, 'Whatever makes me happy.' How great is he?"

Charli opens the next book of wedding photos and refuses to comment. She grunts and flips through the album. I ignore the grunt because I understand what it means. She thinks Jack and I are moving too fast. I try to explain to her how long we've loved each other, how far back this goes. It's like we've wasted so much time, and now we finally get to act on our feelings.

Jan has already expressed her concerns; she thinks I need to 'focus on me.' She doesn't get it, I am focused on me. This is what I want, not what I'm being told or led to do. Haven't these people ever been madly in love?

Anyhow, I am doing stuff for me. I'm taking a business course online. I half run the shop for Charli now, but even though she has dropped hints about retiring for good and selling me the business, I'm still not quite ready to own a flower shop. The thought of all that responsibility overwhelms me. Besides, Jack says it's all up to me, I can work, stay home, do a little of both, he's happy if I'm happy. What's more perfect than that?

THIRTY-FOUR *HAVENWOOD CONDOMINIUMS*

8:00 P.M.

"Hey Kadee-bear. I missed you."

"Hi, Daddy. Bye Mommy see you Sunday."

"Bye, honey, love you. Don't forget to brush your teeth before bed."

"Relax, Liv, I'll remind her. You said in your text you wanted to talk to me about something?"

I watch the back of her little blonde head, ponytail swishing until she rounds the corner. Assumedly, she's gone into the living room to watch TV. I've never stepped inside the condo; it would be too weird. She didn't even bat an eye when I said I'd be dropping her off instead of

Daddy picking her up, like he usually does. I should be glad, yet I worry that she's suppressing her feelings and holding back questions, that she's afraid to upset anyone.

She's always been so agreeable, like me. Part of me wants her to rebel, stomp her feet and pout. Yet another thing I must discuss with her father, but first, the engagement. Jack's proposal had been sudden and entirely unexpected, but very romantic and sweet. Kadee took the news pretty well and even asked if she was going to be a flower girl or a bridesmaid. I didn't even realize she knew that much about weddings.

Her father is a different story. I've been dreading this, but it can't be put off any longer. This could set back our progress, upset the fragile truce we've built over the past year. But there's no putting it off.

"Yeah, I did — I do, that is. Listen, uh, I wanted you to hear this from me first. Jack and I—"

"You're getting married."

He says it like a statement, a dull monotone. He's unsurprised, but I see him flinch as if stung. After everything that's happened between us, I still somehow feel guilty and badly for him.

"Yes. I wasn't expecting — he, well, it was a surprise."

258

"Little fast, no? Sorry, forget I said that. None of my business. Long as you're — as long as Kadee is happy, right? She knows about it?"

"Yeah, yes. Thank you, and I get it. It's sudden. Kadee seems fine. You'll let me know if she says otherwise?"

"Yeah, yeah, sure. No problem."

"You, uh, remember what the therapist said, right? No leading questions? Just let her talk when she feels like it? Not that —"

"Yeah, Liv, I know. I remember what the asshole, Dr. Frank the Freak show said. Sorry, I really don't like the guy in our business, ya know?"

This is a bone of contention for all three of us. Kadee doesn't like 'Dr. Frank' or his stupid hand puppets or 'feelings friends' and neither do her father and I. Still, it seems like the right thing to do in light of the fact that she is now a child of divorce. I'm not sure if I'll ever not feel guilty for that. Dr. Frank certainly doesn't help with his, 'children of broken homes' talks. Asshole is right. We should take her to someone else, I suppose. Or not at all.

"Okay, well, I should be going. You'll call or text of Kadee needs anything, yes? Otherwise, see you Sunday?"

"Yeah, sure, sure. We'll be fine, Liv. See you Sunday. Oh, and congratulations."

Before I can respond, he's closed the door. From behind the wood facade I hear him making lion roar sounds and Kadee giggling. The upside to the divorce has been that he has become an actual hands-on parent, so there's good to be found here.

THIRTY-FIVE *LIVVY TAKES THE LONG WAY HOME*

8:27 P.M.

The downside is the guilt. The constant nagging guilt coupled with the second guessing of everything I say and do with Kadee. I am terrified of messing her up, making her a damaged human because of my choices. What if she grows up not trusting men, or the sacred institute of marriage? Or me? Two marriages before the age of thirty. What message does that send to a little girl? I can only imagine what people think of me.

I try not to care, but I hear things. I'm the gossip of our old street, they all believe Jack and I were carrying on while Brad and I were still married. I mean, they're not entirely wrong, so that deepens the shame. Somehow, the guy who was a mentally abusive bully comes out looking like the victim. How does that even happen? Suddenly, I realize I have a death grip on the steering wheel and my shoulders are tensed all the way up to my ears.

Exhale. Slow down, Livvy. I realize that out of old habit, I am taking the long way home. Only now, I have a home I want to get to, so that's silly. At the last moment, I decide to cut through Marshall Road. I haven't been on this road since we moved, and I find myself slowing down as I pass the old house. I'm self-conscious as I do, I don't want the old neighbors to see me, but most of them wouldn't recognize the Black SUV I now drive. A gift from Jack.

The new owners have made a few subtle changes, adding rose bushes and removing the hydrangeas I'd lovingly pruned. To each their own, I guess. But otherwise, it looks the same from the outside. Of course, it's been less than a year since it sold, so why would I expect otherwise? I can't but help wonder if they've kept the garden, or Kadee's old swing set. I sigh. What am I doing? There's a sweet handsome man at home waiting for me. He's texted twice, asking if I'm alright.

If this had been Bradley, it'd have been angry texts with all capital letters, but with Jack, it's all worry and concern. He's sensitive like that, always checking if I'm happy, if I need anything, if I'm all right. Sure, sometimes it's a bit much, but he means well, so I can't get mad at him.

Furthermore, he'd waited so patiently in the shadows for me the whole time, never pushing and always understanding. I honestly don't know how I got so lucky. I can't help but smile as I pull in the driveway. It's beginning to get dark out, and the porch light has turned on.

The climbing rose bushes have been trained along the arched entryway and along the porch railing and the delicate red blooms burst from the lush green carpet of leaves, ornamental grasses spring up in feathery mounds along the stone walkway, giving the house a beach cottage feel. Exactly the way I wanted it to. Jack, unlike Bradley, actually listens to me.

Of course, no one is perfect. The only mistake Jack made was in hiring a landscaper to do the work, rather than letting me do it myself, as I'd intended. He meant it as a surprise, thinking I'd be pleased, so didn't have the heart to say anything. Trivial things like that roll off my shoulders, it would be mean and ungrateful to criticize his good intentions, so I say nothing. I can see him through the living room window, moving about the kitchen, his shirt sleeves rolled up to his forearms. I'll bet he's got the stereo on, classical music, or smooth jazz, anticipating my arrival. A repeat of last week when he proposed.

Not without a sense of Deja Vu, I walked in to the house, set my keys and purse on the foyer table and quietly stepped into the kitchen. Though the floor plan is open, making me easily visible, Jack's back was turned, and the music is up high. He'd poured two glasses of wine, set on a tray with brie, crackers, and grapes. Out in the backyard, through the open French doors, he'd lit a fire.

A perfectly romantic evening all planned for me, by a man who asked nothing in return but my love. He startles slightly when I say, "No Macy tonight? I thought she was with us this weekend."

"Nope, Paige called, requested the presence of her daughter at a 'mother-daughter paint night', or something like that. Macy wasn't thrilled, but she went like a good girl."

"I see. Yes, those painting parties are the thing these days. I've gone with Jan and the ladies a couple of times."

"Ah, how is Jan? Christian? Don't forget to invite them to the clam bake, it's the Weller summer tradition. Oh, and Barb and Ted, as well. And your parents, too."

Another thing Bradley would never do — throw parties. Jack's reminded me to invite Jan, Mary, and the rest of my friends at least half a dozen times already, even though

I've told him I've done so. I love that he tries so hard to tie our lives together and knows how important my friends are to me.

"Yes, yes, and Mary and Bob, Karla, and the Martinez's, and Katie and Liz. Don't worry, they're all coming."

"Good. I want everything to be perfect. Oh, and about the clam bake, I have something I'd like to run by you."

He looks like a boy who has been told the greatest secret ever and can barely contain it. What on earth is he so excited about.

"What would you say to the idea of surprising everyone with a wedding? At the party, I mean."

I'm stunned. A surprise wedding? In three weeks? No wonder he's been so adamant about inviting everyone; this isn't a new thought, he's been thinking about it for a while now. Everything is moving so fast, I've barely adjusted to being divorced... and engaged again. Olivia Weller. It sounds so nice together. So much for keeping my maiden name. Jack looks so hopeful, so sincere that I find it impossible to let him down.

"Really, Jack? You really want to do this? There's so much we have to do, how will we ever be ready in time?"

"Livvy, sweetheart, if that's a yes then don't worry about a thing. I'll take care of the details; you pick out whatever you want for flowers, dresses, decoration... anything you want."

"Oh, my goodness, I can't believe I'm saying this, but, yes. Let's do it..."

It would be a lie if I said I don't worry that this is a mistake. But we're in love, we're happy, and we've waiting so long to be together that it must be right. It feels right. Mostly. The old Livvy, the one before Bradley, wouldn't be afraid. She would follow her heart. So that's what I do.

"Here, take your wine. Let's toast. Oh, but, how thoughtless of me. How did it go with Bradley? I was worried about you, you know."

"Ah, yes. You should just hand me the whole bottle. Kidding, it was fine, I think."

I'm not really in the mood to discuss Bradley after Jack's gone to the obvious pains of setting up this ideal scene, so I change the subject.

THIRTY-SIX *DONE DEAL*

1:48 A.M.

Two weeks and one day later, I am Mrs. Olivia Weller. It is our first night as man and wife. The moonlight shines through the open bedroom window, falling over Jack's bed — our bed — where he sleeps soundly. My husband. The summer heat caused him to cast off his shirt during the night, kick off the covers and expose his bare skin. We both prefer fresh air over air conditioning, but tonight is excessively warm. I let my eyes travel down his naked body, unabashed now that he was asleep. Such a handsome, sweet man.

I'm tempted to press my own naked body against his, rouse him from sleep to make love again, but the heat has made my skin damn with a fine sheen of sweat and I feel more thirsty than sexy. So instead, I opt for a sheer nightgown and a trip to the kitchen for water. I don't bother with a robe. None of the kids are here since we leave for our honeymoon cruise in a matter of hours.

I take my glass out onto the deck and survey the mess that is the backyard. Red plastic cups and checkered paper plates litter the yard, the lights around the Tiki bar are still lit, and the long family style dining table still has steamer pots and dinner remnants from end to end. The votives that ran down the center have burnt down to nothing and the flowers have begun to wilt. Thank God Jack's hired a cleaning crew to come in the morning.

The clam-bake-turned-surprise-wedding was a success. The only ones who knew beforehand were Charli and Jan. Jack was disappointed that I'd told them, even offering to do everything that I'd have asked them do, but I explained that I wanted to include Jan and Charli. It was actually our first disagreement. Finally, he admitted that he was afraid they would try to dissuade me, causing my frustration to vanish instantly, and I reassured him that it wouldn't happen.

Sometimes I want to remind Jack that he doesn't have to do everything for me, that I can do things myself, but he looks so pleased and proud that I can't bear to hurt his feelings. He'll calm down as time goes on, I'm sure. Even if he doesn't, there are worse things than a guy who is too nice. Of course, not if you ask his ex-wife Paige. It was inevitable that she and I would cross paths, especially since I started going to Macy's soccer games and bringing her to her practices when she was with us.

Surprisingly, she wasn't the tense hostile woman I remembered, or that Jack described. In fact, she was rather nice in a snarky, sarcastic way, the kind of woman whose compliments were always a bit back handed.

"Well, good for Jack. Finally found himself a woman that'll put up with him. You're a young one, though, aren't you? It's that Jack Weller charm isn't it? That's how he sucks you in, and then... well, you'll see for yourself."

I admit, part of me wanted Paige to explain what she meant, and I also wanted her to shut up. Having my image of Jack sullied by his ex-wife is absurd. Of course, her opinion would be negative. The second wife had followed her career out of state, and since they'd had no children, they had no reason to stay in touch, giving no opportunity to gather her current feelings toward Jack. He has only said that they were incompatible and realized it quickly after the married. The split was amicable and quick, and his daughters never even mentioned her.

Paige is nice to me and didn't seem to have any real grudge. I'm not even sure if she remembers me from the daycare center, nor do I feel compelled to remind her. When we see one another, we manage a friendly, superficial banter and I deflect and avoid her overtures to discuss Jack. I had wished he were there to help me but work often has him swamped with blueprints and plans.

Thinking of his blueprints and plans reminds me to check his office door to make sure it's closed. Cowboy has a habit of running in there and stealing Jack's storage tubes and chewing them to bits. Sure enough, it's open. Funny, I never feel compelled to snoop in Jack's office like I did with Bradley. Jack is like an open book, always sharing, always present — both physically and emotionally. In fact, I've never known anyone who's as attuned and attentive as he is.

Attentive enough to notice my wants and wishes, and my habits and quirks as well. It was Jack who pointed out that I swore a lot — a habit I'd been oblivious of — and was an unfortunate side effect from life with Bradley, I suppose. Nonetheless, he was right, and I've curbed the profanity quite a bit. Around him, at least. I appreciate that he's old fashioned and likes for his girlfr— his wife, I mean — to behave a certain way. Most importantly, he doesn't tell me what to do, he asks nicely. Unlike Bradley, who gave orders.

"There you are. I woke up, and you were gone. I thought for a minute I'd only dreamt you."

"Oh, Jack, you startled me. No, silly man. I am real as real can be. The heat woke me. Or perhaps it was all that alcohol. Ugh."

"You should've woken me. After all, it is my job as your husband to take care of you. Shall I close the windows and turn the air on?"

"No, and no thank you. It's our job to take care of *each other*, and we'll be leaving in a few hours anyhow. No need to put the air on. Why don't you go back up and rest for a bit longer? I'm going to put on a pot of coffee and wait for the sun to come up. I'm too excited about the cruise to fall asleep now, anyhow."

"Are you sure? We had quite a busy day, you really should try to sleep at least until six. Or I could sit up with you if you'd like?"

"Jack. I am completely certain, I'm wide awake, and I can see that you are practically sleepwalking. Go on up, I'll wake you when it's time to get moving."

Jack leans down and kisses the top of my head and shuffles back upstairs. For the millionth time I think, 'How lucky am I?' If he weren't so consistent in his actions and behavior, I'd think he was too good to be true, but he is always so protective and chivalrous, not to mention kind and loving. I can actually see the love in his eyes when he looks at me as if I am a precious gift he can't believe is his.

Sure, Bradley's kind of love was intense as well. But that was a possessive and controlling version of love. He wanted to own the things he loved where Jack wants to love and be loved. It's the same thing I've always wanted: to be loved and cherished, trusted and respected. Jack does all of that and so much more. We are going to have a good life together. The kids will all meld, and we will be a big happy family, something I've also always wanted. Now,

I have it — all of it. The handsome, loving husband, the beautiful children and home. A dog running around our fenced-in yard, a job I love doing. I have everything I have ever dreamed of, everything that I thought Bradley and I should've had.

Thinking of him gives me a slight twinge of guilt. I don't want to feel bad for him, I want to continue hating him. But the minute I signed those divorce papers, the ever-present tension and constant pressure dissipated and deflated. Across the long table in a small room of the courthouse sat the man who was no longer my husband. Fifty pounds lighter, all the meanness knocked out of him, and unable to pick his head up when the judge declared the marriage officially dissolved from that day forward.

He was, in that moment, a broken man, and I was the one who broke him. I wanted to feel elated and vindicated. I thought I'd do a victory dance and celebrate, and though I did feel those things, I also felt sad and sorry for him, for us, for Kadee. This was a life, and a future wiped away with the stroke of a pen, and it was as surreal as the marriage now felt. Enough of that. Bradley is no longer my problem. Maybe the guilt I feel for altering Kadee's life will ever go away, but I don't have to feel it for

Bradley. This is on him, not me. Now, wait, I mean both of us. We both did a fine job of it.

Anyhow, Kadee mentioned that Daddy has a girlfriend now, so there's hope he'll finally stop giving me those sad puppy eyes and making me feel bad for being happy. Frankly, I'll be thrilled if he does. The sooner he moves on and finds happiness, the better for all of us.

TWO YEARS LATER

JULY

THIRTY-SEVEN *KADEE'S BIRTHDAY*

1:30 P.M.

"Brad, Krista. Come on in. So glad you guys could make it. Kadee's in the living room, decorating. She wanted to do it all herself, so… well, you'll see for yourself."

"Hey kid, thanks for inviting us, I really appreciate you including us. Listen, can I talk to you for a second before we go in there? Kris, you don't mind, do you?"

"Nope, go for it. We brought wine for you and Jack, I'll go put it in the kitchen? And how about I take that big boy off your hands and bring him in to his Daddy?"

"Aww, thank you, that'd be great. This guy feels like two years going on ten for as heavy as he is. Go see Krista, Max."

"Come on, little big man. Let's go bring wine to your Daddy."

Another one of those surreal moments. My ex-husband's girlfriend carries my son by my new husband out of the room. Like it's totally normal. I turn back to Brad, who is watching Krista and Max until they've gone out of sight. I still get anxious whenever Brad says he wants to talk, old habits die hard, even after several years of being divorced.

"What's up, Brad? If it's about the recital tickets, I swear, they're only giving four per kid so tell Rita it wasn't a deliberate snub. This time."

"Ha, ha, no it's not that. It's uh, well, I'm going to ask Krista to marry me and, well, I wanted you to be first to hear."

I'm not actually surprised. In fact, I told him a year ago he needs to marry the woman. She's perfect for him, straight forward, no nonsense, and best of all, she keeps him in check. Something I could never do. Kadee seems to like her, more so than she's ever liked Jack, to be honest.

I'm not sure if Bradley is seeking my approval or just giving me a heads up, but I give him a quick hug and congratulate him, adding an 'it's about time' dig.

"How are things with you and Jack these days?"

"Eh, you know, the usual." I shrug, casting a guilty glance over my shoulder in the direction of the kitchen where Jack can be heard giving a dissertation of red wine pairings to a politely attentive Krista. It's probably not appropriate to discuss my problems with my new husband to my old one, but he'd caught me in an off moment a few months back, and well, now the cat's out of the bag, so to speak.

Truth is, I'm having serious doubts about having married Jack. A couple years in, and I'm feeling smothered again. This time it's not with domineering and possessive behavior, but in kindness and attention. What the hell is wrong with me? Who gets disgusted by being very loved? Me, apparently.

"Well, Livvy, I don't want to get in your personal business, but you should talk to him. You know, tell him to back off."

"Yeah, well, how well did that work with you?"

Instantly I regret saying that, but Bradley takes it in stride and owns it.

"Liv, I was a fucking asshole. Jack's a good guy. A bit of a pussy, but a good guy. I had to learn my lesson the hard way — by losing you, my family."

Well, this is awkward and uncomfortable. Bradley being contrite. Never thought I'd see the day, yet here it is. Jack has a hard time understanding how I am able to be so friendly with Bradley, but it's simple. I do it for Kadee.

I don't let myself think about how awful he was during our marriage and the first half of the divorce proceedings, I think about how happy Kadee is to have everyone together and not fighting or acting tense.

Just at the right moment, Kadee bursts in to the room, announcing that everyone needs to come see her handiwork in the living room. We all make the appropriate 'oohs' and 'ahhs' and Kadee beams. This is why I make every effort to get along with Bradley and invite him to Kadee's birthday parties.

"Here's a glass of wine, my love."

"Oh, actually Jack, I was going to have — never mind. Thank you."

Jesus Christ, I wish he'd stop trying to anticipate my every desire. I've tried telling him a thousand times, he doesn't have to do everything for me. What used to be sweet and thoughtful, now is cloying. From the corner of my eye, I see Bradley smirking. He's secretly pleased that Jack and I are struggling right now. Well, I am struggling. Jack acts oblivious — slow blinking at me when I say to him *relax, let me do things*. He cocks his head like Cowboy when I ask him to stop hovering.

I hear myself. I think I sound like an ungrateful bitch, but last month, when I finally said as much to Jan, she shouted, "Finally, you see it."

"What. What does that mean? You think he's, like—"

"That means I think he's like a Stage Five Clinger, that's what it means. He always has been, but you were so, 'Oh isn't he so sweet,' and 'Oh, isn't he so thoughtful', who could tell you otherwise?"

"It's not like I haven't asked him to stop. He doesn't listen. I feel terrible for getting so frustrated with him, and I want him to, I don't know, I want him to—"

"Grow a set, maybe? I dunno, just saying. Jack went from being that Hot Daycare Dad to I-wanna-be-your-sugar-Daddy in a hot minute."

"Ugh, yes, exactly. At least he's nothing like Bradley. That's something."

"Are you kidding me? Liv, he is like the nice twin to Bradley Handler. Happy Pants used to try to control you by outright telling you what to do. Sappy Pants smothers you into submission. Different means, same result. You attract these guys that want to *own* you. They think you're a fragile little butterfly and they want to put you under glass and preserve you. Is that what you want? Whatever happened to finishing that online business course? The floral design seminar? Take over the flower shop? Charli is still waiting for you to take the reins, so she can finally retire, you know."

I left Jan's house angry. Didn't talk to her for three whole days. I didn't tell her I was mad, but I'm sure she knew. She's wrong, I thought. Bullshit. Jack is nothing like Bradley. How could she even say something so absurd? But after, I couldn't stop replaying our conversation over in my head. Could she be right? Is this another type of controlling behavior? A subtler one, of course, but controlling nonetheless?

The fact is, I did blow off the online course. I had one more test to take, and I'd have been done. But then Jack proposed, and we got married so quickly, and well, the pressure was off. That's the real truth. I was on my way to independence and self-sufficiency, never mind single parenting, and yes, I was scared. I was on the verge of renting a condo, just me, Kadee, and our divorce guilt gift, Cowboy. It was the only major one I allowed myself to do.

Charli was preparing me to take over the flower shop, still is technically, but now she's let me know that if I don't decide soon, she's going to shut down entirely at the end of summer next year. I want it, I really do, but I've yet to broach the subject with Jack yet. Jack. Dear, sweet, clingy, overwhelming Jack. He swooped in as I started to teeter totter, offered me respite from all the worrying and stress of doing everything alone. 'We already know we love each other, why postpone our happiness together any longer,' he said.

It made sense at the time. But now, I can't help but wonder what would have happened to us if we'd waited, and simply dated for a time. Would we have lasted, or would we eventually gone our separate ways? I suspect I know the answer, but when I look at Max, our beautiful boy, I can't imagine any other path.

Just as Kadee is the spitting image of me, Max is the clone of Jack. To Jack's credit, he never behaved as though he longed for a son, for concern that it would hurt his three daughter's feelings, but when we found out we were having a boy, tears of joy welled in his eyes. I loved him so, in that moment. When did it start to change? It's hard to say, really.

Initially, I'd brought Max to the flower shop, as I'd done with Kadee years before. However, Max was more of a handful than Kadee had been and I soon realized it wasn't going to work. I expected Jack to balk at the idea of putting Max in daycare, but instead, he offered to adjust his work schedule to stay home with him while I worked. I was relieved and pleased, and of course, grateful. However, I also felt a little guilty, as well. I had stayed home with Kadee the first two years of her life, and here I was, leaving Max for hours at a time, several days a week at only six months old. Sure, he was with his Dad, and at home, but he wasn't with me.

Naturally, as soon as I got home, I wanted to spend time with Max, lavish his chunky cheeks with kisses and hold him in my arms, but I began to notice Jack would become petulant and outright whiny when I did. He was jealous of the love and attention I was giving to our son. As surprising and irritating as I found it, I tried to appease him by being more attentive to him as well, just assuming I was in the wrong and being neglectful of my husband.

He also expected almost constant praise and acknowledgement of his helpfulness, something that at first was easy and natural to do. But as with everything else, he went over the top. If I said I wanted to make a special family dinner, he'd have it all prepared the moment I got home. If I told him I'd finish the laundry that night, it was done and folded. Okay, that one was nice. But it had gotten to the point where I'd stopped telling him what I wanted or planned to do anymore. I couldn't help but remember once wondering how anyone could get tired of someone being nice to them and realizing that now I see. It's not the niceness, it's the neediness behind it. The approval seeking, the excessiveness. The clinging. Sometimes I think that if he could crawl up under my skin, he would. I can't understand his type of insecurity. He's one of the most handsome men I'd ever known, both his ex-wives were beautiful, I'd consider myself pretty alright, too.

Clearly, women are attracted to him, so why does he feel the need to cling to tightly? I don't need to ask his first wife, Paige what she meant that day at Macy's soccer practice; I see what it was that drove her and the second one away, his personality.

I don't want to feel this way about Jack. I want to keep seeing him as the Hot Daycare Dad, the man all the girls were smitten with, the guy with the slow sexy smile and lean build. He still looks like that. In fact, he looks better than most men half his age. But I've seen too much. I know differently. Underneath that handsome veneer lived a very insecure, needy man. I see now that he exhausted his daughters, Macy was so glad to have someone else on the receiving end of his attention, it was no wonder she welcomed me into her life with such open arms.

Tonight, after the party, I will tell him my plans with the flower shop. I'm not worried about him trying to stop me; I'm concerned he'll try to join me. Somehow, I'll have to let him down gently, so I don't hurt his fragile feelings.

THIRTY-EIGHT *THAT WAS EASY*

8:20 A.M.

I am in a wonderful mood this morning. When I told Jack about the flower shop, it went better than expected. I was so certain that I was going to have to tell him he couldn't work with me in the shop that I was stunned when he merely hugged me and said what a wonderful idea. He even offered to build an addition to the back room, so I could have a playroom for Max whenever he was there with me. An idea I couldn't refuse, of course.

"Good morning, beautiful. I made you coffee."

"Thanks, Jack. Good morning to you, too."

"So, I was thinking, when we add the playroom, we might as well expand that workroom, too. Maybe section off some office space so I can do paperwork and whatnot in a separate area from the work shop. We wouldn't want to get in each other's way all the time, would we?. Of course, that's all pending building and zoning board approval. But don't you worry your pretty little head about that. I've already put in a call to my buddy Bob over at the town, and I'll have some prints drawn up by the end of the day. Okay, gotta run. This is going to be great. Love you, sweetheart."

Jack kisses the top of my head and dashes out the bedroom door before I have a chance to respond. I call 'wait' after him, but the front door has already opened and closed before the word is out. *No. No, no, no.* This is not the plan, not what I said last night. Not even close. He took for granted that I wanted his help that I needed his help. I should never have agreed to let him add the play room; that was his 'in.' Darn it. No, you know what? Fuck. Fucking, fuck, fuck.

AUGUST

THIRTY-NINE *FINE MESS*

3:30 P.M.

"Is it too early for wine?"

"Well, it's five o'clock somewhere, right? Grab a couple glasses, I'll pour, you talk."

"Thanks, Jan. Uh, keep pouring. That's better. So, ya, I could use some advice on how to handle this whole Jack-thinks-he's-going-to-partner-with-me in the flower shop problem."

"Oh, Jesus fucking Christ. I'll tell you what to do: you tell him no fucking way, right? If you don't, then you're a chickenshit. Serious, Liv, if you want him to stay the hell out of there, you gotta tell him. Otherwise he's going to be in there every damn second, all up in your business, and I don't mean flower business. And what the hell, doesn't he have a job already? A pretty good one at that?"

"Yes, he does. He's a partner, so he can work from wherever he wants, technically. He wants to build an addition to the back of the shop, a playroom for Max, larger work room for me, and an office for him. He's already gotten the approval from the town. Pays to have connections, I guess."

"I guess so. Well, what do *you* want, Liv? I mean really? What? You haven't been happy for, like, the past year. I think it's safe to say it's not that post-partum crap. It's sick-of-stage-five-clinger-crap."

Well, there's the million-dollar question, 'What do I want?' Answer, 'I don't freaking know.' I love Jack. I mean, I think I do. I tell this to Jan.

"Liv, do you love him, or the idea of him? He was larger than life to you back then. Now, well, now I think you're seeing that he's just a guy. And not the guy you thought he was. Don't get me wrong, here. I'm not saying you should get a divorce — Lord knows none of us feel like going through that again. But if you're really not happy, then what are you doing?"

"I don't know Jan. I really don't. He is such a great guy. So sweet, so well meaning. But God, he makes me crazy. Last week I was going to paint Max's playroom. I had it all planned out, everything was ready for when we got back from our girls overnight. Oh, by the way, tell Barb I have her straightener when you see her later. Anyhow, I was ready to go, and when I got home Jack pulls me down the hall, all excited like, and says, 'ta-daaaa' as he flings open the playroom door. Son of a bitch painted the room. Completely finished. Well, I lost my shit. I was so mad, I was shaking. I told him, 'Don't you fucking understand? *I* wanted to paint the room, not have it done for me? How can you not understand that? Do you even know me at all?' Ugh, I went on and on, and he stood there like a kicked puppy."

"Well, then what?"

"Then nothing. I apologized for yelling at him. He sulked. That was it."

"And you're okay with that? You're just going to let him take over all of your plans and do all the work for you, so he doesn't pout? Liv, you've gotten a lot stronger over the years, made a lot of strides, but I'm telling you. If you let sad sap manipulate you with his emotions like this, you'll be right back where you were with Bradley. And I mean the pre-divorce Bradley, not Mister Nice Guy Bradley you got now."

"Blech, please don't ever refer to Bradley as being mine to have. He's Krista's problem now."

This makes us both laugh, and Jan agrees to a topic change. After a couple hours of conversation and laughs, I head home. The long way. Jack is home with Max, Kadee is at her Dad's and I need some quiet time to think.

SPRING

FORTY *THE WINDS RETURN*

11 A.M.

Thank God it's spring. Even though it was a mild winter, the shortened daylight hours and lack of green grass or flowers in bloom depressed me more than usual. It's more to do with the situation at home, than anything else. My feelings for Jack have deteriorated at an alarming pace. It was that one question Jan had asked that stuck most predominantly in my mind. Am I in love with Jack, or just the idea of him? I asked myself over and over again and I've come to realize it *is* the idea of Jack I had fallen in love with. And the moment that realization hits me, I am out of love. Just like that.

I try to find it again, really I do. I thought that if I asked Jack for some space, a little breathing room so I could have a chance to miss him, things might improve. I even began sleeping in the family room most nights, so I wouldn't have to feel him watching me as I feign sleep, but instead of backing off, he clings tighter. Its awful to hurt his feelings, but I I've gone so far as to explain that he is smothering me, that his love for me is suffocating mine for him. Still, he squeezes tighter.

Today is the day I am going to ask Jack for a divorce. I feel strangely calm, detached even. I've written out everything I want to say to him, in case he refuses to listen to me, as he has for the past several weeks every time I bring up separating. He is in denial, insisting that 'I'll come around again.' Until now, I have avoided saying the words, 'I am not in love with you anymore' because I can't bear to see the hurt on his face if I do. But I also cannot stay where I am unhappy. After Bradley I said that never again would I spent another day miserable in a relationship.

I read once that statistics say people who divorce once are likely to divorce again, the premise being that once you've done it, it's easier to do again. When I heard that, I thought this 'they' was insane. Divorce is miserable, horrible, and awful.

It's every bad feeling you've ever had at once. It turns ordinary people into monsters, makes the most familiar person in the world a stranger. It is vile. Divorce attorneys are skilled at drawing out the worst in human nature, judges make you feel like you are lower than a pile of shit, people who you thought were your friends suddenly act like they don't know you... no one who's ever been through a divorce ever wants to do it again. But then again... yes, it is easier.

Contradictory statements, I'm aware. The thing is, generally, anyone who's gotten divorced, has done so because the marriage was that bad, that wrong, and that unfixable in their mind, that the alternative — divorce and all its ugliness — are a better option than staying married. And once one bad marriage is under the belt, you know you'll never stay in one again. Period. So, if anyone were to ask me, I'd say — if you've never been in my shoes — congratulations. I'm happy for you, really I am. Particularly if you've managed to stay married to a person you love and respect, because I think that's what we're all shooting for when we say I do. I'd also tell anyone who stays in a bad marriage — you're crazy. You deserve more in life, your spouse deserves more, and more than anyone, your kids deserve more. Like an example of what a marriage should look like.

Kadee, as she's gotten older, has been more forthcoming about her feelings. Recently she told me that what she remembers most about mine and her father's marriage was the constant tension in the air. When we separated, and it was her and I in the house, all the tension disappeared, she was relaxed. Then we moved in with Jack. She said it wasn't that she didn't like Jack. He was nice enough, like annoyingly nice (her words) but she simply liked it better when it was just us.

So, I've made a promise to myself on Kadee's behalf. No new men in her life for quite a while. Not that it'll even be on my mind to date. I learned my lesson from jumping in too quickly to a relationship after divorce. I've already agreed to rent Charli's house when she leaves at the end of the summer for South Carolina. Besides, I'll be way to busy with the shop and the kids to even think about dating.

As much as I dread telling Jack that the marriage is over, I've already begun looking forward to my new, independent life. The one I'd intended to start years ago. Jan is right. I have grown a lot. Sure, I slipped a bit when I married Jack so impulsively. I realize my own failings and faults in both marriages. Bradley? Sure, he was awful, but it takes two make a shitty marriage. If we were different kinds of people, we could have balanced each other out instead of drawing out the worst in one another. Proof is in his union with Krista, they fit perfectly. Still, I don't regret any of it, because it would equal saying that I regret my daughter. Same thing with Jack- I don't regret our time together, nor the child we created. None of it was a mistake, just lessons learned, as they say.

"You done daydreaming over there? These flowers aren't going to strip themselves, you know."

"Ha, yes, yes. Present and ready boss."

"Not for much longer, kiddo. In three months, you're the boss. You sure you want all this?"

"Oh, Charli, I couldn't be surer of myself these days if I tried."

"Good. You'll be fine. And I'm always a phone call away if you need me. What about the, uh, other stuff?"

"Tonight's the night. I'm dreading it, but it's the right thing to do."

"Sorry it's all turned out that way. Jack a sweetheart of a guy, but the heart knows what it wants... and what it doesn't want. I'm proud of you, kid."

"For having two failed marriages under my belt before I'm thirty? Thanks, Charli."

"No, you knucklehead. For standing your ground. For not being afraid to do what's hard. For finding your self-confidence. Now, don't you go knocking yourself on account of a couple divorces. There's people who're gonna judge you and criticize you, but they aren't your friends. They don't matter. You do what's right for you no matter what anyone else thinks. The only people you apologize to are the ones you hurt, and after you do that, you move on."

"You ever think of writing an advice column in your retirement? You got some good little nuggets of wisdom, Charli."

"Oh, go on now."

"Charli? Thank you. For everything, for giving me this job, for seeing more in me than I saw in myself, for sticking by me through all my craziness... for giving me the money to get my divorce from Bradley. If you hadn't, my God, I'd still be married to him this day."

"Now, now, that was a loan, and you paid every cent back, like I knew you would. But, you're welcome. I never waste my time on flakes and fools, so safe to say you're neither."

"Tonight is going to be awful. Poor Jack."

"It'd be more awful to keep him in a marriage of convenience. He's a big boy, he'll be fine."

Charli is right. I need to do what's right, even though it's hard. Jack will be fine after the initial shock. Despite my warning him time and again, he still refuses to believe that we are in dire straits. Tonight, I will give him no choice but to believe.

EPILOGUE *WELL, WHAT DO YOU KNOW*

12 P.M.

If I filled a book with all of my most surreal moments in life, this one would be in it. My two ex-husbands standing behind me and my children as we gaze up at a storefront sign:

Livvy's Flowers

Below that, a banner that reads:

Grand Opening.

My flower shop. Jan orders the two men to step aside so she can take a picture of the owner and her shop without her two cronies, and everyone nervously laughs. Ironically, both men consider Jan to be an instigator in both divorces, though neither will say so to her.

Perhaps she did, if by 'instigating' they mean that she encouraged me to not only find myself, but to be true to myself when I did. To be strong, self-sufficient. An insecure

298

man's worst nightmare. But here we all are, unconventionally together.

I'm the first to admit that this is not the norm, people don't usually invite their exes to their store's grand opening, but I've never gone the conventional route to anything, so why start now? Of all the self-discovery I've been doing, the most predominant truth is, I need peace and harmony in my life. I have lived unhappy, unfulfilled and untrue to myself. I have made choices out of impulsiveness, weakness and fear, and stayed in situations that were unhealthy for those same reasons.

I have taken the long way, but I am truly home now, and as flaky it this sounds, it turns out home is inside me. I am, in so many ways the same Livvy I always was, but now I am more finely tuned, and the becoming the best Livvy I can be. I'm still getting there. But I am getting there.

Pulling my children in for the photo, I stare out at the people here to support me, my friends, my parents, and my ex-husbands, and I can't help but laugh at it all. This is the moment Jan captures in her picture; it is the one that will hang on the flower shop wall for the next twenty-five years, the one that will watch over a thriving business, a happy life, the wedding planning of my daughter and the transfer of ownership to my son. But that is a long way down the road. Right now, I am living in the moment, cherishing everything, loving my life.

ABOUT THE AUTHOR

Elsa Kurt is a multi-genre, author of eight contemporary women's novels. Livvy Takes the Long Way, Lost and Found Girls, The Awkward Woman's Guide To Dating, Still Here, The Writer's Romance, Books one and two in the Welcome to Chance Series, Mae's Café and A Season To Remember. She is also the author of the YA fiction novel Into the Everwood (Book One) and motivational/inspirational companion book, Finding Beauty in the Imperfections of Life. Her most recent undertaking has been a presentation, course, and a book for aspiring and new writers called You Wrote It, Now What? Elsa has also written several children's books under the name Melanie Cherniack, all with themes of encouragement, empowerment & uplifting messaging.

She has two novellas published with Crave Publishing as part of their Craving: Country Anthology & Craving: Loyalty Anthology, and a third, collaborative anthology titled, Craving: Billions available fall of 2018. She is also working on Book Two of her Everwood Series, yet to be titled, as well as a prequel to Lost & Found Girls, titled Finders Keepers.

Elsa is a happily married mother of two grown daughters and resides in New England. Elsa can be found on social media:
https://facebook.com/authorelsakurt/
https://instagram.com/authorelsakurt/
https://twitter.com/authorelsakurt
https://www.goodreads.com/author/show/15177316.Elsa_Kurt
https://allauthor.com/profile/elsakurt/
https://amazon.com/author/elsakurt and her website,
http://www.elsakurt.com

If you enjoyed Livvy Takes the Long Way, please consider giving it a review on either Amazon or Goodreads. Reviews help the author & other readers find new books.

ARE YOU IN A BOOK CLUB?

If you're interested in having Elsa as your guest author, you may contact her at authorelsakurt@gmail.com.

Please see the following pages for book discussion suggestions.

BOOK DISCUSSION QUESTIONS:

1. What did you like best about this book?

2. What did you like least about this book?

3. What other books did this remind you of?

4. Which characters in the book did you like best?

5. Which characters did you like least?

6. If you were making a movie of this book, who would you cast?

7. Share a favorite quote from the book. Why did this quote stand out?

8. What other books by this author have you read? How did they compare to this book?

9. Would you read another book by this author? Why or why not?

10. What feelings did this book evoke for you?

11. What did you think of the book's length? If it's too long, what would you cut? If too short, what would you add?

12. What songs does this book make you think of? Create a book group playlist together!

13. If you got the chance to ask the author of this book one question, what would it be?

14. Which character in the book would you most like to meet?

15. What do you think the author's purpose was in writing this book? What ideas was he or she trying to get across?

16. How original and unique was this book?

17. If you could hear this same story from another person's point of view, who would you choose?

18. Which places in the book would you most like to visit?

19. What do you think of the book's title? How does it relate to the book's contents? What other title might you choose?

20. What do you think of the book's cover? How well does it convey what the book is about?

*Questions compiled from: https://bookriot.com/2017/08/21/book-club-discussion-questions/

CPSIA information can be obtained
at www.ICGtesting.com
Printed in the USA
BVHW041144170419
545798BV00012B/84/P

9 781733 753937